Ishmael looked around again. The utter alienness of the too-dark blue sky, the Brobdingnagian and blood-red sun, the salt-thick sea, the shaking land, the bloodsucking palsied vegetation and the air aswarm with floating animals and plants gripped his heart and squeezed it.

He thought about where he could be. The *Rachel* had been sailing on the nocturnal surface of the South Seas in 1842, and events indicative of unnatural forces had manifested themselves. And then, as if the sea had been instantly removed, the ship had fallen.

As if the sea had been removed. What if the sea had been taken away, not by magic but by evaporation? By Time's evaporation?

He was convinced that he was on the bottom of the dried-up South Pacific. The dead sea was all that was left of the once seemingly boundless waters. . . .

THE WIND WHALES OF ISHMAEL

THE WIND WHALES OF ISHMAEL

PHILIP JOSÉ FARMER

SF
ace books

A Division of Charter Communications Inc.
A GROSSET & DUNLAP COMPANY
51 Madison Avenue
New York, New York 10010

ONE MAN SURVIVED.

The great white whale with its strange passenger, and the strangled monomaniac its trailer, had dived deeply. The whaling ship was on its last, its vertical, voyage. Even the hand with the hammer and the hawk with its wing nailed to the mast were gone to the deeps, and the ocean had smoothed out the tracks of man with all the dexterity of billions of years of practice. The one man thrown from the boat swam about, knowing that he would soon go down to join his fellows.

And then the black bubble, the last gasp of the sinking ship, burst. Out of the bubble the coffin-canoe of Queequeg soared, like a porpoise diving into the sky, and fell back, rolled, steadied, and then bobbed gently. The porpoise had become a black bottle containing a message of hope.

Buoyed up by that coffin, he floated for a day and a night on a soft and dirge-like sea. On the second day, the devious-cruising *Rachel*, in her retracing search after her missing children, found another orphan.

Captain Gardiner thought Ishmael's story the strangest he had ever heard, and he had heard many. But he had agonizing business to press and little time to wonder. And so the *Rachel* sailed on her crazy path, looking for the whaling boat containing the captain's little son. The day passed, and the night rushed over the sea, and lanterns were lighted. The full moon arose

5

and turned the smooth waters to patches of sable and sparkle.

The coffin-buoy of Queequeg had been raised to the deck, and there Captain Gardiner had walked around it, eyeing it queerly, examining from time to time the strange carvings on its lid while Ishmael told his story.

"Aye, I wonder what the heathen savage wrote when he fashioned these," the captain muttered. "Curious that an unlettered wild man should make these letters. A prayer to one of his Baal-like gods? A letter to some being he thinks dwells in the otherworld? Or perhaps these form words which, if uttered, would open the gateway to some clime or time that we Christians would find very uncomfortable indeed."

Ishmael remembered these speculations. In after times he wondered if the captain, with his last remark, had not struck deep into the lungs of the truth. Were the twisted carvings which began to slide and melt if looked at too intently the outlines of a key that could turn the tumblers of time?

But Ishmael did not have much time to think. Captain Gardiner, in consideration of the strain through which he had gone, allowed him to sleep for the rest of the day and half of the night. Then he was awakened and sent aloft to the head of t'gallant mast to watch and so earn his keep. With the lantern blazing at his back, he scanned the sea which, having lost all movement, lay like quicksilver around the *Rachel*. The wind was dead and so boats had been put out ahead of the *Rachel* to pull her along, and the only sound was the splashing of the oars as the men strained and an occasional grunt from a sweating sailor. The air seemed as heavy as the sea, and indeed it had assumed a silvery and heavy shroud. The moon was full, drifting through a cloudless sky as if through a sluggish stream.

Suddenly the hairs on the back of Ishmael's neck, so

accustomed these last few days to this reaction, stood on end. The tips of the yardarms ahead and below seemed to be haunted with the ghosts of fire. And each of the three-pointed lightning rods seemed to burn. He turned and looked behind him, and the tips of the yardarms spouted phantom flames.

"St. Elmo's fire!" a cry arose.

Ishmael remembered that other ship and wondered if this, too, were doomed. Had he been saved only to be killed shortly thereafter?

The men in the boats quit rowing when they saw the giant candles of the elemental fire, but the officers in the bows of their boats urged them back to their work.

Captain Gardiner shouted up, "Ishmael, my man, do you see any sign of the lost boat?"

"Nay, Captain Gardiner!" Ishmael shouted back down to him, it seeming to him that his breath made the nearest taper waver as if it were a candle of genuine fire. "Nay, I can see nothing—as yet!"

But a moment later he started and gripped the narrow railing before him. Something to the starboard had moved. It was long and black, and for a moment he thought that it surely must be the boat, perhaps half a mile away. But he did not cry out, wanting to make sure and so not gladden the captain only to destroy his happiness. Thirty seconds later, the black object lengthened out, cutting the mercury-colored sea with furrows of a lighter silver. Now it looked like a sea serpent, and it was so long and slender that he thought it must be that beast of which he had heard much and seen nothing. Or perhaps it was the tentacle of a kraken surfaced for some reason known only to itself.

But the black snaky thing suddenly disappeared. He rubbed his eyes and wondered if the exhaustion of the three days' chase of the white whale and the ramming and sinking of the ship and a day and a night and half a day of floating on top of a coffin had made him forever after subject to disorders of the brain.

Another lookout cried out then, "A sea snake!"

Other cries arose, even from the men in the towing boats, who were not able to see nearly as far as the men on the masts.

From every quarter, long thin black things writhed and spun and slid over the black-and-silver waters. They seemed destined to drive their lancelike heads into the sides of the hull of the *Rachel*, and then to evaporate. At first there were only a dozen; then there were two dozen and soon there were several hundred.

"What are they?" Captain Gardiner shouted.

"I do not know, Captain, but I don't particularly care for them!" the second mate shouted back.

"Are they interfering with your rowing?" the captain said.

"Only to the extent that the men cannot keep their mind on their work!"

"They may do what they wish with their minds!" Captain Gardiner bellowed. "But their backs belong to me! Bend to your oars, men! Whatever those things are, they cannot hurt you any more than the corposants!"

"Aye, aye, sir!" the second mate called back, though not cheerily. "All right, men, you heard the captain! Dig in your blades and pull! Pay no attention to those mirages! Ah, that is what they are, mirages of the sea! Phantoms, reflections of things that don't exist! Or, if they do, so far away they can't hurt you!"

The dip of the oars and the grunting of the men was heard again over the still waters and still air. But now the serpentine "mirages" began to circle, as if they were trying to catch up with their own tails and swallow them. Around and around they went, cutting deeper

8

and brighter furrows in the sea, or seeming to do so. And the corposants, the St. Elmo's fire, on the tips of the yardarms and the trines of the lightning rods, seemed to burn more fiercely. They were no longer phantoms but living creatures whose breath was hot.

Ishmael moved away from them, pressing his legs and stomach against the hard railing and looking straight ahead, not wanting to look directly at either of the flames which flanked him.

There was a shriek from below, and a man ran into a hatch as a flame twice as tall as a man, and bifurcated, capered after him.

At the same time, the forward tips of the long black circling objects in the sea spouted St. Elmo's fire. They were like those snaky whales of prehistoric times, the fathers of the present-day round monsters, blowing out spouts of flaming brimstone.

Ishmael looked to left and right and saw that the tapers at each tip of the yardarm had split and that one of each pair was dancing along the yardarm toward him.

Ishmael grabbed the railing and closed his eyes tightly.

The captain shouted, "Lord have mercy on us! The sea has come alive, and the ship is burning!"

Ishmael dared not open his eyes but he also dared not remain in ignorance of what was happening. He saw that the ocean surface was a maze of whirling broken circles of black with a flaming jet at each end. The ship itself, at every point where any object projected upward more than several inches, was crowned with a flame which no longer danced but gyrated. Around and around the flames whirled. And the corposants which had been doing the minuet toward him had leaped while his eyes were closed and fused directly above his head. He could not see all of them, because they leaned when he bent his head to look at them and so most of their "body"—if they could be said to have a "body"—stayed out of reach of his eyes. But enough light shone from them so that he could see their outer surface, and he knew a moment later, on looking down at the officers and crew, that the corposants were gyrating on top of his head, a slender toe of fire almost touching the crown of his head.

The dark circling things on the ocean had joined and formed a writhing spiderweb. Illuminated by the thousands of coldly burning tapers at the corners where the snakes had joined, the sea looked like a cracked mirror.

Ishmael felt that the world was indeed cracking and that the pieces would fall on his head any moment.

It was a terrifying feeling, one that drove him to pray out loud, which even the events of the last three days on the *Pequod* had not made him do.

The flames went out.

The black web disappeared.

There was utter silence.

No man dared say a word or even sigh. Each feared that if he brought the attention of whatever force it was that crouched above them, he would bring something down that would be worse than death.

A wind blew in from the west, rippling the sea, fluttering the sails, then pushing them.

The *Rachel* heeled to starboard; the wind passed; the *Rachel* righted herself.

Silence again.

The silence and the agony of waiting were beaten out into a thin wire of apprehension.

What was coming?

Ishmael wondered if he had been spared from the horrible but quick doom of the men of the *Pequod* for something unimaginably dreadful. Something that God might imagine but would repress in His mind.

What followed could be recalled afterward only because he, Ishmael, could look back and reconstruct. So that he did not so much remember as imagine. At the time, he could not possibly have known what was happening. All was strangeness and horror.

With no more noise than of a ghost gliding over the ocean, the sea disappeared.

Night was replaced by day.

The *Rachel* was falling.

Ishmael was too terrified to cry out, or, if he did cry out, he was too stunned to hear himself.

Falling through air, the *Rachel* turned over quickly, the weight of the masts and sails revolving her to starboard because she had been leaning very slightly in that direction when the sea evaporated so quickly.

As if shot from a sling, Ishmael went out into the abyss and then was sinking through the whistling sea of atmosphere by the side of the ship. He waved his arms and kicked his feet as if he were trying to swim.

The moon was with them, though its companion, night, had deserted it. But the moon was enormous, fully three times as large, perhaps four times as large, as that he had known.

The sun was at its zenith. It was a sullenly red ball that had swelled fourfold.

The sky was a dark blue.

The air screamed past him and through him.

Below him—no, below the *Rachel*—was a strange craft sailing through the air.

He had no time to learn anything but its alienness and the sensation that it had been built by intelligence. He did see some human beings running about it, and then the tip of the mainmast of the *Rachel* crashed into

11

it, and the rest of the ship followed, and the strange vessel of the air broke in two.

Perhaps a hundred feet below the two vessels, and below him, was what he had thought was the top of the mountain. It was a vast russet-streaked, mushroom-colored thing which was the plateau-land of the peak of a mountain that towered miles high.

He struck it, was hurt, and passed through a layer of something like thin flesh.

Again and again, he struck a layer and tore through it, each time feeling a jar that hurt but each time being slowed.

Then something ropy flashed by. He grabbed for it, missed, felt another ropy thing slide through his hands, burning them. He cried out, plunged on through layer after layer, struck something solid that exploded like a balloon, deafening him and filling his nose and burning his eyes with a choking and burning gas.

His hands closed on something he could not see.

He swung out, far out, almost losing his grip. He blinked his eyes to wash out the pain with tears. Then he swung back and, still swiftly, but not fatally, fell at the end of a pulpy root attached to a corpse-colored bladder which was flesh or plant or a mixture thereof.

He was still breaking through paper-thin skins. He understood, without thinking about it, that there were thousands of bladders of many sizes that must hold up the thing, whatever it was.

The last layer broke beneath his feet so reluctantly that he thought for a moment that he would have to kick through it. He feared to keep on falling, but he feared even more being stranded inside this fragile, treacherous being.

Then he went through the hole, the bladder which he was holding sticking for a moment before his weight pulled it through with a tearing of a skin layer. He was below a vast cloudlike mass of russet streaks and mushroom-pale tissue. Below him was the edge of a dark blue sea and a jungle. The *Rachel* had struck the sea and split into a hundred parts, which were lying on top of the sea as if it were made of a jelly. The parts of the airship had not yet fallen to the sea. In fact, one part, being carried by the wind further because, he supposed, it was lighter, would land somewhere in the jungle near the sea. The other would land about half a mile beyond the *Rachel*.

Before he had fallen another mile—or so he estimated, though he had no way of knowing for sure—he saw the first smash into and then be swallowed up by the jungle. It was as if the vegetation had crawled over it after it had crashed.

The second and smaller half struck the surface of the sea hard enough to split it into a dozen parts. Some rebounded and floated westward for a considerable distance before settling down again.

He wondered if he was falling swiftly enough to be smashed against the waters.

It was then that he saw that he was not alone in the sky.

So far away that he could determine only that it was human, but not its features or its sex, another figure, clinging to the ropy snout of a flesh-colored bladder, was also falling slowly.

Something indefinable made him think that the other survivor was not of the crew of the *Rachel*.

The other person was higher than he, which meant that he had fallen later than Ishmael. Or perhaps his bladder was larger than Ishmael's.

During one of his swings, for he was like a pendulum whose energy is decaying, he looked upward past the round of the balloon-bladder. Near the center of the vast mass were several huge holes torn by the bulks of the *Rachel* and the two parts of the airship. The holes that he and the other being had made were invisible.

A moment later he struck the surface of the ocean feet first. He went completely under and came up choking. The water stung his eyes strongly; what he swallowed seemed almost solid with salt.

The bladder had burst on impact, being carried into the water with him. The gas made him cough even more and his eyes felt as if a white-hot blade had been passed before them.

He found that he did not have to swim or make any special efforts to keep floating. This was a sea even deader than the Dead Sea of Palestine or the Great Salt Lake of Utah. He could lie on his back and look up at the great limburger-cheese-colored moon and the enormous red wheel of the sun and not have to move a muscle.

Yet, though thick with the minerals, the waters moved with a current. The current was not, however, with the wind but against it. And it was not a steady current. It was formed with the sluggish waves that wandered westward and did not seem to be of the nature of waves he knew. Though he was too numb with terror, past and present, to do much analyzing or speculating, he did feel that the waves were more those of the land than of the sea. That is, they were generated by earthquakes.

Then that strange thought passed, and he slept. Lifted up and lowered gently, moved slowly but irresistibly to the west, face up, arms crossed (though he did not know that until he awoke) he slept.

When consciousness returned, the sun had not descended much from the zenith, though he felt as if he had slept eight hours or more.

Something bumping into his head had brought him out of a sleep deep in dreams that circled his wounded mind like sharks around a man thrashing in the water.

He reached up and pushed himself away, sliding only a foot or so in the stiffly yielding waters. Then he swam to one side and found that he had collided with Quee-queg's coffin-buoy. It floated with only an inch or two draft and seemed to say, "Here I am again, your burial boat, also undestroyed by the fall."

With an effort that left him gasping, he hauled himself up on top of the box, the carvings allowing him a purchase for his fingertips. The coffin settled down a few more inches. Lying with his chin against the edge, he reached down on both sides and paddled toward the shore. After a while, tiring, he slept again. When he awoke, he saw that the great moon had moved far, but that the sun had not advanced more than a few degrees.

The vast cloudlike creature through which he had plunged, and one of whose organs he had torn out, was gone. But in the west another one loomed. This was much lower than the first, and, when it got closer, he could see that hordes of strange creatures with wings like sails were tearing at it.

There were many different types of eaters, but there were several kinds, similar yet distinguishable, which he came to call air sharks. Since they were about five thousand feet high, they could not at that time be seen in detail. But a later meeting enabled him to see them much more closely than he cared to.

The smallest of the species was about two feet long; the largest, eight to ten feet. All were scarlet-skinned. All had heads which were enormous in relation to their bodies. These were torpedo-shaped, and the mouths were split far back with rows on rows of tiny white triangular teeth. The top of the head bulged out as if internal pressure were about to blow it up and scatter the brains, if any, for yards around. The analogy was not exaggerated, since the top did contain a bladder filled with lighter-than-air gas. There was also a huge hump on the body just back of the head, the two humps creating a dromedary effect that was more sinister than comforting. No man would care to ride between those hump bulges.

The body was shark-shaped, and the skin that covered the fragile bones was very thin. When one of the creatures got between Ishmael and the sun, its skeleton and internal organs would be silhouetted.

The end of the tail had two vertical fins more like a ship's rudder than a fish's fin. Both extended so far that they looked heavy enough to drag the air shark's tail down, but they, too, had diaphanous skin and thin bones.

The beasts apparently were dependent upon the wind for their main means of locomotion, though they could propel themselves somewhat with a sidewise motion of the tail that enabled the tail fins to be used as a shark's. The double pair of very long wings, like a dragonfly's, that extended from just behind the head, could be rotated almost 360 degrees and raised and lowered slowly. The black-and-white checked appendages were more sails than wings. But the beasts knew by instinct how to sail close-hauled against the wind, how to tack, how to do all the maneuvers that human sailors have to be taught.

The great russet-and-mushroom-colored cloud-creature swept overhead, harried and eaten alive—if it was alive—by the multitude of air sharks. Then it was gone to the east, blown toward the line of purple mountains far away.

Ishmael did not know why the first cloud-creature had been undisturbed by the scarlet check-winged predators and the second attracted so many. But he was glad that they had been absent when he had been born into this world.

He lay on his back while the coffin-canoe lifted and lowered with the quakes passing through the heavy waters. After a while, he saw another vast cloud, but this was pale red, and its outlines changed shape and area so swiftly that he doubted it was anything but a peculiar cloud. And why not peculiar? Was not everything in this world bound to be peculiar, except himself? And from the viewpoint of this world, was he also peculiar?

When it passed over him, a tentacle, or a pseudopod—it was too blunt and shapeless to be a tentacle—put out from the cloud toward the earth. The sun shone through it so that it looked more like a beam of dust motes than a living thing.

A few pieces of the pseudopod drifted by him and separated into tiny objects. They did not come close enough for a detailed examination by him. But against the dark blue sky the red things looked many-angled in the lower part. The upper part was umbrella-shaped and doubtless acted as a parachute.

Other creatures followed the vast red cloud as bats follow a cloud of insects or as whales follow a cloud of brit, the tiny creatures that compose the bedrock of all sea life and are swallowed and strained out of sea water by the mighty right whales.

Indeed, that analogy was not exaggerated. The monstrous things that spread their fin-sails and plowed into the red cloud, their giant mouths wide open, must be the right whales of the air of this world.

They were too high for Ishmael to have described them with particularity. But they were enormous, far larger than the sperm whale. Their bodies were shaped like cigars, and the heads, like the sharks', were so large they were almost a second body. The ends of their tails supported horizontal and vertical fin-rudders.

The wind took cloud and cloud-eaters out of his sight.

The sun descended, but so slowly that he feared this world would come to an end before its sun touched the horizon.

The air became hotter. When he had first crawled up onto the coffin-buoy, he had thought that the air was just a little too chilly to be comfortable. When he had awakened, he had thought that the heat was a little too much to be comfortable.

Now he was sweating, and his throat and lips were dry. The air seemed to lack moisture, though it was directly above the sea. And the shore was still so distant that he could not see it. He could only float or assist the natural drift with his hands. He began to paddle, but this increased his rate of sweating and, after a while, he was panting. He lay face-down with his chin on the edge of the coffin, and then he turned over. Another great red shape-shifting cloud was far overhead with its attendant leviathans of the atmosphere.

He began paddling again. After about fifteen minutes he saw land ahead, and this renewed his strength. But hours passed, with the sun seemingly determined to ride forever in the daytime sky. He slept again and when he awoke the west was definitely a coast with vegetation. Also, his lungs were turning to dust and his tongue to stone.

Despite his weakness, he began paddling again. If he did not get to the shore soon he would end up dead on top of the coffin instead of inside it, where he would properly belong.

The shoreline remained as far away as ever. Or so it seemed to him. Everything in this world, except for the creatures of the wind, crept painfully and maddeningly. Time itself, as he had thought once when on the *Pequod*, now held long breaths with keen suspense.

But even this world of the gigantic red sun could only delay time for so long. The last of the sea waves deposited the fore-end of the coffin upon the shore.

Ishmael slipped off the coffin onto his knees, up to his groin in the thick water, and felt himself rise and then subside with the swell of the sea-bottom. And, when he staggered onto the land and pulled the coffin-canoe the rest of the way out of the water, he felt the ground quake under him.

The shimmying made him sick.

He closed his eyes while he picked up one end of the coffin and dragged it into the jungle.

After a while, knowing that the earth was not going to quit trembling and quit waxing and waning, he opened his eyes.

It took a long time to get used to the earth being a bowlful of jelly and to the palsied plants.

Creepers were everywhere on the ground and in the air. These varied in size from those as thick as his wrist to those large enough for him to have stood within if they had been hollow. Out of them sprang hard, fibrous, dark brown or pale red or light yellow stems. These sometimes grew up to twenty feet high. Some were bare poles, but out of the side of others grew horizontal branches and tremendous leaves big enough to be hammocks. They kept themselves from sagging by putting out at their free ends tendrils that snagged neighboring stems and then grew around and around them. In fact, every plant seemed to depend upon its neighbors for support.

There were also a variety of hairy pods, dark red, pale green, oyster white, and varying from the size of his fist to that of his head.

He could find no water, though he described a spiral

through the jungle and then returned to the seaside. The ground under the creepers was as hard and dry as that of the Sahara Desert.

He studied the plants, wondering where they got their moisture, since they had no roots into the earth. After a while it occurred to him that the bare stems rising into the air might be the roots. These could gather whatever moisture was in the atmosphere. But where did the vegetation get its food?

While he was pondering that, he heard a chirruping sound. Then two pairs of long fuzzy antennae slid out from behind a leaf, and a globular head with two huge lidless eyes followed. From the feelers and the head, he had expected the rest of the body to be insectlike. But it was bipedal, and the neck, chest and two hands were definitely mammalian, monkey-shaped and covered with a pinkish fuzz beneath which was a pale red skin. The legs and feet were bearlike.

The animal was two feet high and, in the light of the red sun, its two insectlike pincers were revealed as outwardly curved double noses. The lips underneath were quite human; the teeth were those of a carnivore.

Ishmael felt threatened. The creature could inflict a nasty bite which, for all he knew, might be poisonous.

It did not, however, offer to attack him. It cocked its head while its antennae vibrated and then, still chirruping, flashed away into the jungle. A moment later, Ishmael saw it seated on a branch, where it was tearing a large pale-green pod from its stalk. The creature turned the pod until a spot, darker green than the rest of the pod, was visible. It jabbed a rigid finger at the spot, and the finger sank in. The beast pulled the finger out and then inserted one of its noses into the hole. Evidently it was drinking.

After it had emptied the pod, it squatted immobile so long that Ishmael thought it had gone to sleep. The lidless eyes became dull, and a film crept over them. Ishmael, feeling it safe to approach, discovered that the film was a semiopaque liquid, not a lid. He also saw that a thin, pale green creeper had lifted itself and moved up the beast's back and entered its jugular vein. The creeper became a dull red.

After a while, the creeper delicately and slowly removed its tip, reddened with blood, from the vein. It withdrew snakishly down the creature's back and slid into a hole in the stem out of which it had come.

The eyes of the beast lost the milky film, it chirruped feebly and then it stirred. Becoming aware that Ishmael was standing so close, it ran into the jungle. But it had not moved as swiftly as before.

Ishmael had been about to imitate the creature and stick his finger into a dark spot in a pod and drink from it. But now he feared to do so. Was there something in the water that temporarily paralyzed the drinker? And did a creeper come out and tap the drinker's vein every time? Was this a strange symbiosis, sinister to him but only natural in its ecology?

There was, of course, nothing to prevent him from tearing off a pod and running into the sea, where a creeper could not get at him while he drank.

But what if the water contained some drug which would paralyze more than his body? What if it were a sort of *lotos,* which would so influence him that he would return to the jungle and invite the bloodsucker to feast on him?

While he stood in indecision and his body ached for the water so available yet so remote, he saw a number of creepers slide out from many holes in stems. They converged on the pod, covered it, exuded a greenish slime which cut through the shell of the pod, and presently each creeper withdrew with a section of shell held in a coil at its end.

No wonder the earth was so bare. The plants ate of their own substance. No doubt they also ate anything else that was dead. And the food they needed over and above their own detritus was provided by blood.

Acting quickly, so that he would not get to thinking too much of the possible consequences, he tore a pod loose. He turned and ran until he was standing in the sea up to his thighs. He tilted the pod above his head and let the water run out into his mouth. The liquid was cool and sweet but there was not enough. There was nothing else to do but return and break off another pod.

As he started back, he saw a shadow flash by him, and he spun around and looked upward.

In the distance was still another great red cloud with its devouring attendants, the wind whales.

But the shadow had come from something much nearer. An air shark had sped over him at about thirty feet from the ground, and behind it were three more.

The first two had made a surveillance pass, but the last two in line had decided that it was safe to attack him.

They dived toward him, the wing-fins changing their angle, and their great mouths open.

He waited until the first was within six feet. It was then only a foot above the water, and it was hissing.

That mouth looked as if it could not miss biting off his head, which must be what it planned to do. It surely could not snatch him into the air, and if it landed it would be at a disadvantage in the water. Or would it?

Ishmael went completely under, his eyes and mouth closed and his fingers pinching his nose. He counted to ten and emerged just as the lower tail-fin of the last air shark trailed by him, dragging in the water.

Getting out would have been swifter in less thick water and if he had not been so fatigued. He thrust his legs forward while he looked to his left and then he was on the narrow beach, diving into the shelter of the jungle.

The beasts had lifted slightly and were sailing close-hauled to the wind. They cut at an angle away from him out over the lake for a quarter of a mile. Then they turned and sailed at an angle toward the west, and then turned again, their wings rotated to catch the wind in full.

Ishmael tore off a pod and punched a hole with his finger and drank. The excitement and danger had made him forget his caution, and that, he thought a minute later, was his undoing.

The first time he had drunk, he had not felt the paralysis he'd expected. He had been braced to step forward so that if he became so paralyzed he fell, he would fall with his face out of water. He had felt nothing. But this might have been because he was so much larger than the double-nosed beast; much more of the narcotic in the water would be needed. Also, the excitement from the sharks may have counteracted the effect he should have felt.

But two drinks in such rapid succession did their work. He immediately felt numbed and could not move. He could see, though through a twilight, and he could feel the creeper slithering up his back and a dull pain when the sharp end penetrated his jugular.

The air sharks swept over him, having spotted his head projecting above the vegetation. He had made a mistake by picking this place to drink when he could have chosen one with much higher and much more dense plants.

However, the beasts were necessarily cautious. They came close the first time but did not try anything. Doubtless they were trying to estimate the chances of getting caught in the vegetation if they tried for a bite.

He did not fully understand how they operated. Bladder gas made them buoyant, he was sure of that. And it seemed to him that they could not lose much altitude without discharging gas. That might be the hissing noise which had come from the first shark.

To gain any altitude, they would have to use the same tactics as gliding birds. And if they were to stay aloft they would have to generate more gas. To do this, they would have to use something in their bodies. Fuel was necessary, and to get fuel, they had to eat. That much should be certain, if anything in this world was certain.

Theorizing was fine, in its place. What he needed was to act, and he could not move.

It seemed a long time before the sharks appeared again far to the windward and turned onto the final leg of their maneuver. The heat had built up; the vegetation cut down most of the wind. He was sweating, and the first insect he had seen scuttled out on a branch a foot away.

It was the representative of an ancient and successful line, a breed that had learned to live *with* and *off* man. It even put out to sea with man and was much more successful at its parasitism than the rat.

It was a cockroach, at least nine inches long.

It crept out cautiously, its antennae wiggling, and presently it was on his shoulder. Its familiarity showed that it was acquainted with the paralyzing effects of the pod-water.

He could not feel its legs on his skin, but he could feel a dull pain on the lobe of his right ear.

He should have drowned with the crew of the *Pequod*.

There was a rustle—his hearing wasn't dulled—and he was staring at a face that had appeared from behind a mass of leaves.

The face was as brown-skinned as that of a Tahitian maiden. The eyes were extraordinarily, almost inhumanly, large, and were a bright green. The features were beautiful.

The language she spoke, however, was none that he had ever heard, and he had heard most of the world's languages.

She stepped forward and batted at the cockroach, which sprang onto a branch and disappeared.

At the same time, he felt the end of the creeper withdrawing.

He had expected her to pull the creeper out, since she had rescued him from the insect. She, however, went after the huge thing with a stick and in a minute returned holding it by several of its legs. It was still kicking, but its guts were oozing out of a big crack across its back.

She held the thing up and smiled and spoke melodiously. He tried to open his mouth to reply but could not. Evidently she knew he would not reply, because she sat down and began to hack the creeper open with a stone knife.

Ishmael had forgotten, though only for a moment, that the sharks were swooping at him. Now he tried to open his mouth to shout a warning. Perhaps she could push him over so that the plants would keep them off him. Or she could . . .

The girl must have sensed that he was warning her. His eyes were rolling in terror. She stood up and turned and looked up just as the first shadow fell. She screamed and jumped back, bumping into him and toppling him over backward. His head struck something. He awoke to feel the earth, as always, trembling beneath him and rising and falling as if there were a tiny tide sweeping through it. That might not be so farfetched, he mused. Actually, on the earth he had known, the ground did rise and fall, pulled by the moon and the sun. But it was such a small phenomenon that man never noticed it.

Here, where the moon and the sun were so enormous, earthtides were detected even by the most insensitive.

He felt sick at his stomach. Either the sucking of his blood had been accompanied by an injection of some poison or he would have to reaccustom himself to the quivering of the land.

He tried to sit up and found that his hands and feet were tied.

The girl was gone.

Apparently she was not as friendly as she had first appeared. She had not seemed anxious about him then because she knew he was unable to hurt her.

He did not blame her, since he was a stranger and she would have been a fool to have approached him without caution. Perhaps she would not have been a fool, though, if she lived in a world where human beings were friends and murder and war were unknown.

That she had bound him showed that she did not live in such a utopia.

He sighed. It was too much to expect of any world that human beings should all love and trust each other. As on Earth, so here. So every place, probably. Fortunately, Ishmael did not have to be in a utopia or seeking one to be at ease.

He was not at ease now, of course. But he felt relieved and even optimistic. He was not the only human being in this world, and once he learned the girl's language, he would get answers to some of his questions.

Ishmael smiled at her as she expertly butchered a double-nosed monkey-bear beast. While she worked, he inspected her closely. She wore a large white comb of some ivory-like substance in her hair, which was as long and free and black as any maiden's of Typee. Her ears were pierced to hold thin rings of some jet-black stony material in each of which was set a large dark green stone. This stone bore in its interior a bright red object that looked like a spider.

Around her neck was a ruff of short feathers of many colors, and around her waist was a thin, semitransparent belt of tanned leather. On the lower end of the belt were bone hooks which supported a kilt that ended just above the knees and was of the same material as the belt. Her sandals, of a thick dark brown leather, encased feet with four toes, the little toe having been exiled by edict of Evolution.

Her figure was slim. Her face was definitely triangular. The forehead was high and wide. The enormous luminous green eyes were shadowed by eyebrows excessively thick and black but arched by nature. The lashes were tiny spears. The cheekbones were high and broad but still less wide than the forehead. The lower jaw angled inward, ending in a chin which he would have expected to be pointed but which was rounded. It was the chin that saved her from ugliness and carried her off to beauty. The mouth was full and pleasant, even when she began to bite off pieces of the animal's fat.

Ishmael, having seen many savages who ate raw meat, and having himself indulged, was not repulsed. And when she offered him a large piece of meat, he accepted with thanks and a smile.

Both ate until their stomachs were packed tightly. The girl found a stone and cracked open the animal's skull and dug out the brains and ate this. Ishmael might have accepted her offer to this, if he had been starving. But he shook his head and said, "No, thanks."

Apparently shaking the head meant to her a positive, because she started to feed him. Ishmael, sensitive to the contrary way of alien people, understood his error at once and nodded. She looked puzzled, but she withdrew the food.

There was no disposal problem, he saw. She had only to carry the bones and other matter to the nearest plant and beat with her hand on the plant. Within a few seconds, a creeper emerged from a small hole in the stem and wrapped itself around the remains. Other creepers, as if notified by some vegetable telegraph, slid out of other holes and also enfolded the carcass.

The girl tore off six pods and punched two and drained one into Ishmael's mouth. During this procedure, the creepers ignored them. He supposed that this was because they had been given meat and blood and so had spared the giver. Nevertheless, the water numbed both him and the girl for about fifteen minutes. During this time, if any predator had appeared, it could have had them with no more effort than it took to leisurely gnaw away upon them.

When he was free of his paralysis, Ishmael tried with rolling his eyes and squirming his body to indicate that she should untie him. She frowned, very prettily, he thought, and sat for a while considering his desires. Then she arose and, smiling, cut the intertwined grasses with which she had bound him. He arose slowly, rubbing his hands and then bending over to rub his feet. She backed away, the knife in her hand, but after a minute decided that she must go all the way or not at all. She put the knife into a scabbard of leather on her belt and turned her back to him.

He climbed upon a plant leaning at forty-five degrees to the ground and looked out over the jungle. As far as he could see, there was vegetation except on the top of some seemingly very high buttes in the distance. The whole forest shook as if afflicted with fear.

He himself was tired of the eternal quivering and the faint, but definite, anxiety and slight nausea resulting therefrom. Apparently it did not bother the girl; she must have been born to this form of quaking.

Everywhere except to his right was jungle. On that side was the dead sea, expanding and contracting with the semblance of life.

The air sharks were gone. Far to the west was a broad reddish tinge which he supposed was another of the drifting clouds of tiny objects. With them would come more of the monstrous creatures of the air and perhaps more of the sharks.

The great red sun had rolled some distance down the sky, but it still had a quarter of the heavens to go. The heat had increased, and he felt thirsty again. He dreaded drinking when it meant helplessness for a quarter of an hour. Moreover, what would the cumulative effects of the narcotic be? So far, he had not noticed any headache or particular sluggishness or other results.

He looked down toward the girl. She had climbed into a giant leaf which, hammock-like, was suspended between two thick-boled plants. She was lying down, obviously preparing to go to sleep. He wondered if he was expected to stand guard while she rested or if she just took it for granted that he would crawl into one of the leaves near hers and also sleep. If she had not bothered to inform him of what was expected, then she was not worried. But he could not understand such unconcern. This place held enough known terrors. What of the ones he did not know?

Before lying down to face the question of to dream or not to dream, he looked around again. The utter alienness of the too-dark blue sky, the Brobdingnagian and blood-red sun, the salt-thick sea, the shaking land, the bloodsucking palsied vegetation and the air aswarm with floating animals and plants gripped his heart and squeezed it. He wanted to weep, and he did so.

Afterward, he thought about where he could be. The *Rachel* had been sailing on the nocturnal surface of the South Seas in 1842, and events indicative of unnatural forces had manifested themselves. And then, as if the sea had been instantly removed, the ship had fallen.

As if the sea had been removed. What if the sea *had* been taken away, not by magic but by evaporation? By Time's evaporation?

Ishmael had been a lowly member of the crew of a whaling ship. But that did not mean that he was only a sailor. Between voyages, he was a school teacher and, wherever he was, he read much and deeply. Thus he was acquainted with the theory that the sun would, some day, millions or even billions of years from now—from then, rather—cool from white-hot to red-lukewarm and then become a cold dark cinder. The natural loss of orbital energy would bring the earth closer to the sun. And the moon would draw nearer and nearer to the earth until the mutual attraction, building up, would tear both celestial bodies apart.

Another theory, exactly the contrary, stated that the tidal friction of moon and earth would cause the two bodies to move more and more apart. This theory, according to the graybeard who advanced it, had to be the correct one, and he had proceeded to "prove" it by mathematics. Evidently his mathematics were wrong, or something had happened to interfere with the progression of natural events. Perhaps during his long history man had acquired powers which had enabled him to tamper with even such seemingly untamperable phenomena as the orbits of planets.

Was he indeed on the Earth of the far far future? Had the *Rachel* sailed through a momentarily weakened spot in the fabric of Time or through some conduit of the cosmos, which, operating shutter-like, had opened to take in the *Rachel?*

He was convinced that he was on the bottom of the dried-up South Pacific. The dead sea was all that was left of the once seemingly boundless waters. And the shaking and swelling earth was no fit place for most life. The majority of animals had deserted the ground, filling the area above the ground with aerial fish of various sorts.

Far from feeling even more lonely and alienated with this theory, he felt greatly heartened. The man without a theory or a dogma is ship without sails or rudder. But he who has a theory or a belief has something wherewith to steer by and to sail close-hauled against the wind if need be. He can ride out the roughest of storms and stay clear of shoals.

That he might be on Earth, and not on some planet of some star so distant that no Earth eyes could see it, encouraged him. It was not the Earth he knew, and if he had had a choice, he would perhaps have gone back in Time, not ahead. But he was here. He had not had a home, except for the planet itself, for years; and if he could make himself at home in the forecastle of a whaling ship or among the cannibal Typees, he could try to make a home here.

He climbed down cheerfully and crawled into the leaf-hammock next to the girl. She raised to look at him and then turned her back and apparently went to sleep. There were other leaves above them to hide them from air sharks, but what about the great cockroaches—he fondled his slightly wounded ear—and who knew what other larger and more fearsome carnivores?

What about them? he thought and soon was asleep.

On awakening, he drank more water from one of the pods which the girl had torn off earlier. The sun had now one-eighth of the heavenly arc to go. The heat had increased slightly. The moon had rolled over the eastern horizon like a Titan's bowling ball. At the speed it was going, it would overtake the sun again and both might descend the horizon together.

The girl gestured, and he followed. They crawled around and pushed aside plants until she found breakfast. This was a paralyzed beast which may have been the descendant of the house cat Ishmael had known. Its head could have been Tabby's, but its body was serpentine and the legs were excessively long and thin. The fur was long and shaggy and barred with white and black.

The girl waited until the creeper had withdrawn from the cat's jugular before she stabbed it through the throat. Why she should wait, he did not know. Perhaps there was some sort of mental communication between sentient flesh and semisentient vegetation here. Or perhaps she was merely observing a rule which, if broken, would result in an attack by the plants.

There were many things which he did not understand. But he was glad that he was with her for more reasons than that she was human company. She knew how to fare in this difficult world, and she also seemed to know where she was going. He went with her, since she did not object, and as they traveled northward, he learned her language.

The sun eventually abdicated below the horizon, and a black sky with strange constellations came into succession. The moon, like the death's head of a god, rolled down the heavens. It was so gigantic that Ishmael took a long time getting used to the feeling that it was dropping upon Earth and would crush him. He learned to tell when the large earthtides, following the moon, were coming. He hated these, because they increased that always present—if slight—nausea.

The long, long night was at first hot, then comfortable, then, near the end, cold. He shivered, for he had only a sleeveless shirt and sailor's bellbottoms; his shoes had been carried off while he slept by, he presumed, cockroaches. Namalee, the girl, wore little to protect her from the cold, but she did not seem to suffer at all, being like a naked Patagonian in that respect. It was inevitable that he proposed they sleep with their arms around each other so he could keep warm. She refused, just as later she refused him when he tried to kiss her.

By then he understood her language enough to know at least the name of the place from which she came and why she was here. And he also understood why he was not to touch her.

She was Namalee, daughter of Sennertaa, ruler of the city of Zalarapamtra. Sennertaa was the *jarramua*, which meant king but could be more closely translated into English as the grand admiral. He was also the chief priest of Zoomashmarta, the great god, and superintendent of those who spoke for the lesser gods.

The city of Zalarapamtra was far to the north, halfway up a mountain which Ishmael suspected had once been the undersea half of a South Pacific island. There Namalee lived in a crystalline palace carved by stone tools and by acid secreted by beasts under the guidance of the founder of the city, the demigod Zalarapamtra. She was one of the twenty-four daughters of Sennertaa, who had ten wives. She was a sort of vestal virgin whose chief duty it was to go out with a ship on its maiden voyage to bring it good luck.

Ishmael did not comment on her failure.

She did not seem to be downcast about that. But it was only because a far greater tragedy had obliterated the comparatively small one of the destruction of her ship and its crew.

Several days before the *Rachel* had fallen out of the

33

empty skies, Namalee's ship had met another whaling ship from her city.

The other ship had hailed them, and its captain had come aboard. It was evident that he had horrible news, because his skin was pale and his eyes were red with weeping, and he had applied ashes mixed with grease on his hair and had gashed his breast with a knife and had covered with a mask the face of the little god of the ship.

Namalee had thought at first that her father or mother or the only son of the family had died. The captain's news was far worse than that. The city of Zalarapamtra had been destroyed, and most of its inhabitants killed, in a few hours in the middle of the long night. The Purple Beast of the Stinging Death had done it. Only a few had escaped on ships, and one of these had brought the news to the captain of the whaling ship. He had sailed around and around in his grief until he had found another ship to which he could tell the news.

Tears ran down her face, and she had to hide her face behind her hands for a while before she could continue.

"This Purple Beast," Ishmael said. "What is it?"

"There are fortunately very few," she said. "The half-god, the founder of our city, Zalarapamtra, killed the great Purple Beast that owned the mountain where the city now stands—stood. It is vast, bigger than that tremendous but harmless beast through which we and our ships fell. It trails many thousands of thin tentacles which sting men to death. And it drops eggs which explode with great noise and ruination."

Ishmael lifted his eyebrows at this.

"I am indeed sorry," he said, "that you lost your family and your nation in such a short time and in such a manner. Tell me, are we going north because

Zalarapamtra is there, and you hope to find some survivors and start rebuilding the city?"

"First I have to see for myself what happened," she said. "Perhaps it is not as bad as the captain said. After all, he fled the city during the destruction. He only surmised that everybody had been killed and that the city was totally destroyed.

"In any event, other whaling ships will be returning, and these will be carrying mostly men but each will have one of my sisters. We can make obeisance to our chief god, and promise to obey him better in the future so he will not allow such destruction to come again. And we will elect a new Grand Admiral, and we virgins of Zoomashmarta will take husbands and bear children for the future."

"And your ship was speeding back to Zalarapamtra when mine fell like a wooden star from the heavens and destroyed your vessel," Ishmael said. "I would have thought that blow would have been the last. It's a wonder you have kept your sanity."

He thought about her story for a while, feeling a great pity for her. She was, for all she knew, the last of her family and she might be the last of her nation before the story was ended.

"This *kahamwoodoo*," he said, using the name which, translated, meant the Purple Beast of the Stinging Death, "this *kahamwoodoo* must truly be gigantic. Its tentacles must be very long, too, if they can probe into every room of the city, which you say is carved out of rock and goes deep into the mountain. Surely, though, some must have been able to avoid the stinging death."

"They may have," she said, "but there are some things I did not tell you about the *kahamwoodoo* because I took it for granted that you knew. And I should not

35

have done so, since you are not even of this world, if what you tell me is true."

"It is true," Ishmael said, smiling. He did not blame her for her doubts. If, when he had been sailing with Ahab, he had met a young woman who claimed to have been propelled from the past, would he have believed her?

"The *kahamwoodoo,* according to the stories told by the priests and by the grandmothers, is often accompanied by smaller beasts. These are of various kinds and travel on top of the great beast. When the great one kills, he is sometimes robbed by the smaller, though they dare not take too much. And he does not bother these fellow travelers unless he becomes too hungry or they annoy him. So, you see, the small beasts would have gone into the rooms of the city to kill what the great beast missed."

They were lying on two leaves side by side and over which was a thick canopy of interlacing leaves and vines. Ever since the huge red sun had dropped into the slot of night, she had been particular about having a heavy cover of vegetation over them. She was especially cautious when they prepared a place to sleep. Ishmael had asked her why, and she had replied that there were a number of reasons. She described some of them, and he had trouble getting to sleep thereafter and staying asleep.

This was the second sleep for them that night. He awoke suddenly, feeling a dull pain in his neck. He knew at once that a creeper had inserted its hollow tooth into his jugular. Namalee had told him that the plants went into a semihibernation during the night, but that some awoke enough to search for a victim, just as a sleeping person, half-awake, feeling thirsty, may stumble to the bathroom to get a drink of water. Namalee had advised him that, if this happened, he should submit. It was better to lose some blood than to jerk the tooth free and so fully awaken the plant.

He had asked her why it mattered if the plant was denied its drink. She had replied that it was best to cooperate with the earth growths. She was vague about what might happen if he did not. All she knew was that she had been taught that one should always go along with the arrangement. It was true that a person could avoid the creepers, if one had not drunk the paralyzing water, but it was better to submit.

Ishmael, thinking of the endless miles of jungle through which they would have to travel before coming to the mountain city of Zalarapamtra, decided to submit. He lay with his eyes closed and imagined the drain of blood. The red fluid was oozing through tiny capillaries of the creeper into the body of the parent stem. And then—

He started as he heard a very faint whistling sound somewhere above him. Something bent the tops of the plants, and something shook the vegetation. The rustling he now heard was not the never-ending motion of the plants quivering to the movements of the earth. The rustling was heavier and more prolonged and undoubtedly caused by some great body.

He managed to turn slowly on his side and reach out and swing Namalee's hammock-leaf. The creeper extended itself to compensate for his motion and so leave its tooth in his vein.

Namalee awoke suddenly and sat up, but she did not say anything. Moonlight filtering through spaces here and there enabled him to make out her body as a dim shape, and she could see his hand clearly in a shaft of light. She rolled over to the edge of the leaf very slowly and whispered, "What is it?"

"I don't know," he said. "Something big is out there."

He pointed upward at an angle.

The rustling had increased, and then, straining his eyes, he saw something snakish glide through a lake of moonlight about forty feet away. Namalee, seeing it also, gasped, and said, softly, "The *shivaradoo!*"

The tentacle, which was a dark gray and about an inch thick, was blindly probing. But it was coming closer, sniffing for heat. The *shivaradoo* was blind, like most of the predatory beasts that came out at night, but its sense of heat detection gave it eyes and it had a strange hearing sense that enabled it to pinpoint its victims.

Ishmael plucked the creeper's tooth from his vein, hoping that the forcible ejection would not result in heavy bleeding. He rolled over and eased himself down from the leaf while Namalee did the same from hers. They had to drop a few feet and so could not avoid making some noise. About four seconds later, he heard a sound as of air escaping from pressure, and something pierced a leaf by his shoulder.

Namalee made a strangling sound, and both dropped flat on their faces to the ground. There were about six or seven hisses, and the thud of several objects striking the hard skins of stems.

Immediately after, the two got to their hands and knees and crawled swiftly to a fallen plant with a diameter of two feet. They went over and behind this just in time to escape three more missiles.

Ishmael reached over the trunk and groped until he found a tiny arrow-like thing embedded in the semi-wood. It was a needle-pointed shaft of bone about two inches long and one-sixteenth thick with four featherish growths at the other end. He did not test the sharp end, since Namalee had told him that this was coated with a poison.

According to her, the *shivaradoo* had thirty tentacles, all hollow. The beast grew the bony missiles in its own body. When they were fully developed, they dropped out into a pouch on the underside of its pancake-thin, sixty-feet-diametered body. The *shivaradoo* plucked the missiles out of the pouch with one tentacle and inserted them into the ends of other hollow tentacles. When the *shivaradoo* was close enough to a victim, it expelled a missile with air forced from a bladder-like organ on the top of its body. The range was about sixty feet.

The *shivaradoo*, like most of the creatures of the air, had large bladders of lighter-than-air gas to buoy it. These grew on top of its body.

Ishmael reached over the fallen trunk again to get some more missiles, and he heard hisses, followed by the dancing of leaves through which shafts pierced and the faint thud of more striking into the plant. One had plunged in only an inch from his hand.

Hastily he pulled several out and, holding them carefully, crawled after Namalee.

"It will follow us until it finds us!" Namalee gasped. "And we can't do a thing!"

"You said it could be killed with its own poison?"

"That is what the old tales say!"

They increased their speed on their hands and knees as a crashing noise came from behind them.

"O, Zoomashmarta!" she said. "It's smashing the plants to get at us!"

"It can't come down too far!" he said. "Otherwise, it'll spear itself on the plants! Some of them have pretty sharp points, you know!"

An animal leaped out in front of their faces and caused them to cry out and stop. But it was only one of the *kwishchangas*, the antennaed twin-nosed monkey-bears, as Ishmael called them. Squawking and chirruping, it raced through the middle terrace of the plants and then suddenly fell.

Ishmael could not see what had happened to it, but he supposed that a poisoned dart had killed it.

The jungle was a series of vast snappings and whippings as plants broke or, released of the weight of the passing monster, sprang back to their original positions.

"Zoomashmarta, help us! Zoomashmarta, help us!" Namalee whispered.

The jungle ahead of them was boiling out with life. A horde of the nine-inch-long cockroaches erupted and raced off in all directions. A family of the double-nosed beasts fled up a pole-like plant, each leaping off the end to a branch of a larger growth.

The two, without a word between them, leaped up at the same time and raced through the jungle. They stumbled and fell, helped each other up, and Ishmael dropped his missiles and did not have the time to look for them. But he did take Namalee's stone knife from her.

Suddenly, Namalee stopped. The smaller life was still making its bedlam. But the greater noise of the heavy body smashing its way through the vegetation was gone.

"What is it?" Ishmael said.

"It's lifted and is going slowly now," she said. "Listen!"

Ishmael forced his breathing to slow down and to become quieter by opening his mouth wide and drawing in air in large bagsful. He could make out a susurrus behind them, but it was difficult to hear it through the shrieks and crashings of the smaller animals.

"The *shivaradoo* has no wing-sails, if you will remember," Namalee said. "It travels by seizing the plants with its tentacles and pulling itself along just above the top of the jungle."

Ishmael, who considered this world to be a Pacific of Air, thought of it as a bottom-feeder.

"It intended to flush us out by making a great noise,

and so it tried to crash through to us. But now it will skim just above the roof of this jungle, pulling itself along, and it will go swiftly. More swiftly than we can run through this tangle."

Ishmael had not asked her how the *shivaradoo* ate its prey, but he did so now.

"Why do you want to know?" she said, shivering. "If you are dead, what difference . . . ?"

"Tell me!"

She moved her head from side to side as if she were trying to locate the beast. It must have stopped to listen, because it no longer made a sound.

"It drips an acid on the kill," she whispered, "and this turns the flesh and the bones into a mush which it sucks up through the tentacles."

Ishmael had had a wild idea of throwing some of its poisoned darts into its mouth and so killing it. But this idea was no good now, though it probably would not have been even if the beast had possessed a mouth large enough to have swallowed a man.

"It will drift over us as silently and lightly as a cloud," she said, "its tentacles probing here and there for the heat of our bodies, and its hearing organs alert for the slightest sound. And if we don't run, it will pinpoint us and shoot a dozen darts at once. And if we run again, it will follow us until we are exhausted and then will kill us."

"I wonder how strong those tentacles are?" he said so softly that she could not catch the words. He repeated them and got the expected question, "Why do you want to know?"

"I don't really know myself," he said, and he put a hand on her cold and perspiring skin. "Let me think."

He knew now how a whale must feel. He was down on the bottom, sounding, as it were, while the killer, moving on the surface, waited and watched. Sooner or later, the hunted must make a break for it, and then the hunter would pounce.

The noise of plants bending and of plants being released as the beast started to pull itself along was renewed.

Namalee clung to Ishmael and whispered, "We must run! And if we do . . . !"

"It can't chase us in two different directions," Ishmael said. "I am going to run northward, north by northwest, actually, to take me away from it at an angle. You will count to fifteen after it starts to chase me—not before—and then run southward."

"You are sacrificing yourself for me!" she said. "But why?"

"In my world, where similar situations occur, the male is expected to defend the female in the best manner he knows. That is the principle, at least," he added, "though the practice is often enough the contrary. I haven't the time to discuss the principles or their reason. You do what I say."

Impulsively, he kissed her on the mouth and then he turned and ran as swiftly as he could through the heavy growths.

The noise of the *shivaradoo*'s passage increased.

He ran on until his feet were caught in a tangle of creepers and he pitched headlong onto the ground. In front of him was an especially dense complex of creepers and vines strung over two large fallen plants. He crawled into it, worming and pulling until he was between the logs. He hoped that none of the creepers was in a mood to dine.

The sound of the *shivaradoo* had lessened; it apparently was going more slowly, knowing that its prey had stopped.

Ishmael reached up and snapped off a pod from a stalk. He punched a hole in it but did not drink. He set it by his side and stared through the tangles until he saw the shadowy mass of the *shivaradoo* appear above the jungle top.

The enormous moon glittered on the many minute mica-like particles encrusting its skin. It was indeed as Namalee had described it, a pancake-thin creature with bulges of skin on top which enclosed gas bladders. Its many tentacles moved about, sniffing for heat, while other tentacles clung to the plants beneath it.

After a few seconds, it pulled itself closer. It stopped while the feelers probed around, and then it moved closer again.

Ishmael flattened out even more but kept his head raised. He had to see what it was doing. His heart thudded so hard that he was sure the monster could hear it, and his throat and mouth were as dry as the leaves of an old manuscript in a desert monastery.

And soon as dead—perhaps, he thought.

The beast, having located him, extended six tentacles which, one after the other, shot darts. Each thunked into the log behind which he lay. He counted each and then quickly reached over and jerked two loose before the second barrage came from another six tentacles.

The *shivaradoo* waited for several minutes during which time seemed to be gold-beaten out into a tissue as thin as the film over a snake's eye.

Perhaps it was waiting to determine, by the loss of heat, if it had struck and killed its prey.

Apparently deciding that it had failed, it pulled itself downward until it bent two dozen stems beneath it and then it pulled itself forward. The poles scraped against the lower side without injury to the creature. Poles sprang up and swished leaves and creepers and vines around as it passed them. About twenty feet from Ishmael, the monster was no longer able to force

43

passage. This was to be no deterrent, since it could extend the tentacles on the part nearest Ishmael not only up to him but past him if it wished.

It was cautious now, however. Perhaps because it could detect that its prey was hiding behind a log. Several tentacles lifted and moved out into the air at a height about ten feet above him. Several others slid along the ground, their fore parts raised. Ishmael waited, not sure what he could do. In a minute, both worlds, the ancient—his natal world—and the present—the future—would be lost to him.

Namalee had said that the monster could not expel its darts with any force unless it was through a straightened-out tentacle. A bend considerably decreased the force of the air. This may have explained why it did not shoot immediately. It wanted to be able to use its tentacles as perfectly straight tubes.

Ishmael could hear the whoosh of indrawn air into the bladder which served it as an air tank. It gulped again and again, as it compressed the air.

One tentacle, looking in the moonlight-edged darkness like the trunk of a starved elephant or a headless cobra, moved along the ground ahead of the others. Ishmael had raised his head swiftly, seen it, and then ducked back behind the log. He estimated how soon it would glide over the log and held between two fingers of one hand a dart and in the other hand the stone knife.

Above him, three tentacles curved downward, looking with the blind eyes which saw only the heat of his body. Then one dipped down as if to get close enough so that, even with a considerably reduced charge of air, it could still flick a bone-shaft deep enough to drive its poison into him.

A tentacle curved over the log and stopped. Sniffing

44

for the heat of a living body, it moved back and forth. Then it began to straighten out.

Ishmael rammed the needle point of his dart into the open end of the extension.

Immediately after, he rolled back across the log behind him and into the net of vegetation in back of it.

The tentacle with the dart lodged in it jerked, and Ishmael thought that it swelled. But if it had intended to jet out its own dart, it found itself obstructed. The tentacle jerked this way and that and then coiled back and then straightened out with a snap. This time, both darts were blown out, but they failed to fly more than three feet.

Ishmael rolled back between the two logs, picked up a dart with one hand, leaped up and jumped at the emptied tentacle.

The tentacle retreated, but slowly, as if it were not accustomed to reacting defensively. Ishmael grabbed the tip and this time drove the point of the dart into the soft fleshy part just inside the opening.

The tentacle did react violently then. It dragged him back under the huge disk of the beast, past the fore tentacles. The aft tentacles, which had been facing the other way, perhaps to act as a rear defense, began to turn around toward him.

Ishmael went up the tentacle as if he were climbing a line on the *Pequod*.

His weight pulled it downward hard against the trees.

A dart struck the tentacle just above his head.

The beast was turning its tentacles inward and shooting at him but striking itself.

Ishmael released his hold, fell back about five feet, and crashed into a plant leaning at a forty-five degree angle from the ground. It bent under him until it snapped, and he fell the rest of the way.

The monster abruptly soared, then settled, wobbling,

and grabbed a number of plants and pulled itself away.

Ishmael rolled as far as he could, got to his feet, and ran forward until he was stopped by a net of creepers. He bounced back, fell, got up, and ran around the creepers.

He stopped to look behind him.

A huge mass was settling like a cloud upon the tops of the plants. It seemed to lose its outline and to melt over and down into the jungle.

Ishmael could not clearly see the underside of the *shivaradoo*, but he could detect no movement of the tentacles.

Suddenly, a long torpedo-shape with an enormous head and teeth gleaming whitely in the moonlight shot out of the night.

It bit once at one of the humps on the back of the sagging pancake creature, and the hump exploded.

The air shark, scenting death, had come in swiftly.

Another appeared behind the first and anchored itself by biting into the loose skin of the destroyed hump. It also rotated its wing-fins to eliminate the pressure of the wind on them.

Ishmael wondered if the poison which had killed the *shivaradoo* was strong enough to spread through the body and also kill the air sharks.

He had no time to watch for such a development. He turned around swiftly at a noise behind him. It had sounded as if a large body was trying to move stealthily through the jungle. He got down on his knees and waited with the stone knife. Then he heard a deep and familiar breathing, and he said, softly, "Namalee."

"I could not allow you to sacrifice yourself," she said. "I wanted to help, so . . . oh!"

She had seen the *shivaradoo*, draped over the tree-tops like a cloth.

46

He told her what had happened, and she took his hand and kissed it.

"Zalarapamtra and Zoomashmarta will thank you," she said.

"I could have used their help a moment ago."

They continued walking, skirting the dead beast, which was now being torn at by half a dozen sharks. They walked for hour and then lay down again to sleep. Though very tired, Ishmael kept waking up because of the cold. The end of the night was on them, and the temperature, he estimated, was down to about forty above zero, Fahrenheit.

He tore off a huge leaf and climbed into Namalee's hammock-leaf, wrapped his arms around her, and covered himself and her with the leaf. She did not object, though she did turn her back to him. He went to sleep at once and dreamed of that first night in the Spouter-Inn in New Bedford when the giant savage, Queequeg, had shared his bed. Queequeg, whose bones had turned to dust and become flesh and plant again and again and again. . . .

The tremendous red disk rose slowly again, bringing some warmth immediately. They found themselves being supped off by creepers and waited until the vegetables had had their fill. Then they rose and washed themselves with water from pods and drank. The water paralyzed them as usual, but the creepers, as if knowing that the two had given their share, did not approach them.

They continued north, sleeping four times, catching the twin-noses and cockroaches, which tasted much like crabs, and several other animals, including a flying snake. This was one of the few beasts of the air which lacked a gas bladder. Some of its ribs had developed into great wings which it was able to flap up and down in crude imitation of a bird's wings.

Another night passed with its perils, and another sun arose.

"How long before we reach your city?" Ishmael said.

"I do not know," she said. "By ship, it would take us, I calculate, about twenty days. Perhaps it will take us five times that long."

"About four hundred of the days of my world," he said. He did not groan, because time was not such a precious currency to a whaler. But he would have preferred to ride. It was heavy and exasperating labor to force a path through this dense complex. He envied the beasts that sailed with such seeming effortlessness through the clouds.

At noon of that day, they saw another of the many immense clouds of billions of tiny red animals, each borne by its umbrella-shaped head. And there were the leviathans that followed and fed upon the air brit.

And there was a great ship of the air.

Namalee stood up, dropping the white meat of the insect she had caught only an hour before. She stood silent for a long time after an initial gasp. Then she smiled.

"It is from Zalarapamtra!"

The ship looked like a huge, rather elongated cigar beneath which hung a very thin mast and yardarms and sails and on both sides of which, at right angles to the hull, were two masts and sails. The sails, fore-and-aft rigged, were so thin that the dark-blue sky could be seen through them. At the stern were horizontal and vertical rudders.

"It's not as flat as it looks from here," she said in answer to his question. "If you could see it closer up, you would see that in profile it is twelve men high."

The ship was following a pod of about thirty leviathans, which, spreading out their double pair of dragon-shaped wings, veined with red and black and green and purple, their tremendous cylindrical bodies and huge heads gleaming silver, were driving through the clouds of air brit.

"How . . . ?" Ishmael said, and she put a hand on his arm.

"Watch," she said.

The ship had a full spread of sails. It was traveling swiftly but not swiftly enough to catch up with the whales. Then a smaller object, followed a moment later by another, put out from the big ship.

These were needle-shaped, and the crew lay down in them, Namalee told him, standing only when there was work to be done. The extra rounding on the nose contained a larger bladder than elsewhere. This was necessary because the harpooner stood there when the time came to strike and because the harpoon and its long line were stored there.

He watched as masts were extended above and below the whaleboat and out to both sides. Then the transparent sails were unfurled, and the boat began to speed toward the red cloud.

"How do they manage to drop and furl the sails without going out on the arms?"

"It's done from on board," she said. "The arrangement was invented, so it is said, by Zalarapamtra, but I think that it was used a long time before he was born."

A whaling boat sped on the trail of a leviathan that seemed to be unaware of it. It passed through stratum after stratum of redness, the density of population of the animalcules varying from time to time. It came even with the great beast, and passed on the other side of the red cloud, so that Ishmael could not see it.

Ishmael turned to watch the passing creatures and then he saw the leviathan in the rear of the pod suddenly rise. A silvery sheet fell from it, the ballast of water which it stored in a bladder for two reasons: one, to draw upon when its body needed it; two, for emergencies, when it loosed it to gain levitation swiftly.

Ishmael could see the whaling boat now, connected to the beast by a thin line, one end of which was buried in the head. The wind whale was doing the opposite of sounding; it was soaring for the upper reaches of the heavens.

"It can float for a long time in air in which men would strangle in a short time," Namalee said. "And sometimes a whale is great enough to drag a boat up there, and then the harpooner must cut the line before he becomes too confused to know what he is doing."

The beast had by then taken the boat so high that both were lost in the dark blue. The brit-cloud was northeast of the two watchers on the ground and within half an hour would be touching the horizon. But the ship itself had turned away from the brit and was running close-hauled. Then it turned and was beating against the wind, turned, came back, turned, and was close-hauled again. The maneuvers made it evident that the men on the ship, being much higher than Ishmael, could see the wind whale and its attached boat. And they were still in the general area, vertically speaking, in which the harpoon had first been plunged into the leviathan.

After a while, Ishmael saw the whale as a very small blackish dot. It quickly became larger as it dived, and then the boat became visible. The beast was plunging straight down, its enormous wing-sails folded by its side, its body rigidly straight. The line between hunted and hunter was too thin to be seen. The boat was on a straight line behind and a little to one side of the beast at a distance of about three hundred feet.

"The whale releases its gas quickly and falls," Namalee said. "When it gets close enough to the ground, it will spread its sails and turn upward in a sharp curve. The boat, swinging around and under it, may or may not escape being dashed against the ground. It all depends upon the skill of the whale. Sometimes they err in their estimations of their speed and distance because their wounds have drained the blood from their brains. Then they crash and kill themselves but also kill the boat crew. Of course, the line can be cut before the whale gets too close to the ground, but it is a matter of honor that the harpooner does not sever the line until the very last moment. And sometimes the momentum keeps the boat going, and . . ."

She stopped. The whale, if he kept on at his present velocity and angle, would smash into the earth about half a mile north of them. The animal was now so near that Ishmael could see that this was far huger than any blue whale of his day, which was the greatest animal that had ever lived. The barrel-shaped head was much like its counterpart of the seas of Ishmael's time, but it had no lower jaw. The mouth was a round hole located in the center of the front of the head.

Ishmael asked Namalee about it, and she replied that the creature had no teeth, and its lower jaw was immovable, being grown solidly into the skull. The mouth funneled in the millions of the little red animals and, when the whale's appetite was satisfied, which was seldom, a thin film of skin fell down from inside the mouth to cover the opening.

"But there are whales that have great mouths and movable jaws and these eat the toothless whales and anything else they can, including men," she said.

"I have met such beasts," he said, thinking of the great white whale with the wrinkled forehead and the crooked jaw.

"If that beast doesn't spread its sails and start to turn upward, it will never clear the ground."

Down the gigantic body raced, showing no intention of unfurling sails. All except one of the men in the boat were hidden, doubtless clinging to whatever they used for holds. Only the head of the harpooner was visible. Ishmael expected at any moment to see the arm of the man appear and make a sawing motion with the knife at the line. But the head did not move nor any arm appear.

"Those men are very brave or very foolish," Ishmael murmured in English.

A few seconds later, he spoke in his native tongue again.

"For God's sakes, cut! Cut the line!"

Now the air whale's wing-sails were spread out so suddenly that the crack of the air striking them—or perhaps it was the crack of the great muscles extending the bone and skin of the sails—was like a volley of muskets. The descent of the creature was checked, and its tail, moving downward and jerking the boat about violently, caused it to begin to curve upward. But its initial direction was still maintained, and even though it was now angled upward, it was sinking.

The boat was now below the whale and still swinging from the maneuver which turned the whale upward. Its weight and speed were enough to oscillate it and the huge creature to which it was attached, a case of the mouse shaking the cat, Ishmael thought.

He could see the four men in the boat, three tied to the deck and the harpooner clinging with two hands. The sails had been furled, of course. Though their resistance would have slowed down the whale and tired it, the inevitable dive would have ripped off sails and masts. Even as it was, the masts had bent far under the comparatively little resistance offered by the furled sails.

"It's too late to cut now!" Namalee said. "If the boat is released, it will continue downward! Now all they can do is hang on and hope that the whale will be able to clear the ground enough so that they will not strike it!"

"They won't . . . avoid the ground," Ishmael said.

If the earth had been one foot lower, or the beast had started to turn a few seconds sooner, the boat might have missed. But its aft end struck the earth, and it rotated, the line snapping and the men being thrown out, the harpooner losing his grip and the safety belts of the others breaking. The bones and skin of the boat's structure folded, bent, cracked, snapped, and the vessel bounced several times before disappearing into the jungle.

The whale, having discharged most of its gas, was not able to rise higher than fifty feet after it had leveled off. It would be limited to a low level until it was able to generate enough gas, provided that it had enough food in its stomach to do so. Even then, if it lacked enough food, it could draw upon its own body tissues to generate enough gas to lift it to several hundred feet. If it failed to run across a brit-cloud at this low level—and few clouds came this low—it was doomed. It would sail around, losing gas until it drifted down upon the jungle, crushing the plants under it. And there it would stay while air sharks, various beasts of the ground and the creepers fed upon it.

Ishmael and Namalee pushed through the interweaving growths toward where they thought the men had been thrown. After casting about for some time, they found one. His bones were broken throughout his body; he had been cast through a funnel of vines straight onto the ground. The second man was crying for help.

He lay on a crushed bush and above him were the creepers and vines sheared off by the impact of his body. But he had only a broken leg and many bruises.

The third man was lying in the middle of a great pile of vegetation. He had brought down a whole complex, leaving an empty area in the middle of the jungle. Air sharks, having appeared from nowhere seemingly, were dipping down into the depression and attempting to bite him.

Ishmael and Namalee started to drag him into the shelter of the plants standing at the edge of the cavity. He was half-conscious and groaning. The side of his head was bloodied, as if it had struck a hard-stemmed plant. He wore a kilt of bright blue on which was a black wind whale and a harpoon. A purplish whale was tattooed across his chest and smaller whales to the number of fifty were tattooed down his arms and legs. These indicated the kills he had made during his career.

"He is Chamkri, a great harpooner," she said. "Surely his ship has not heard the news, or it would be speeding homeward, not hunting."

"Here comes a shark," Ishmael said and increased the speed with which he was dragging Chamkri. Then, seeing that the beasts would be on them before they reached the wall of vegetation on the edge of the clearing, he dropped Chamkri. The air shark dipped down over the tops of the trees and folded its wing-sails to its side and glided swiftly downward, gas hissing from a bladder. Ishmael picked up a long bare plant and cut away the vines and creepers wrapped around it. When he saw that the wide jaws were about to close down on him, he thrust the pole deep into the gaping mouth. It drove past the ribbon-like pale yellow tongue and into the throat, and then the mass of the shark knocked him down. The shark slid over him, but only a small part of its weight came down. Nevertheless, his face and hands were bloodied, the creature having a skin almost as sandpapery as its counterpart of the ancient seas.

Namalee shrieked, but she had thrown herself down too, and the shark had passed over her, being deflected by an upthrust of a pile of tangled plants. It crashed into the wall of the clearing and brought down around it another tangle of plants and interlocking vines. It wriggled at first, trying to free itself gently and then, panicking, began to thrash and roll about. It only succeeded in entangling itself even more thoroughly and in breaking one of its wing-sails.

The harpooner having been dragged to safety, Ishmael approached the shark through the jungle. Other sharks swooped over it and snapped at it, but none came close. They dreaded being entangled too, and they never voluntarily settled down on the ground unless their intended meal was dead or helpless and they were free of attack.

Ishmael stepped out by the grounded shark, but not close enough to be struck by the thrashing of the tail. Though the hollowness of the tail and the lightness of its bones meant that the tail lacked massiveness, its abrasive skin was to be avoided. He threw another branchless stem straight into the gaping mouth of a shark diving at him. The jaws closed, and the plant broke in half; the shark swallowed the part in its mouth. Ishmael leaped back into the jungle. A moment later, he saw the beast writhing as if its entrails had been pierced, which was probably the case. The other sharks closed in upon it, biting large pieces of its wing-sails, its tail and its head. The wind carried the dying monster and its raveners out of sight.

Presently two whaling boats descended, tacking, and one settled down into the clearing while the other

stayed fifty feet up, its sails furled and an anchor made
of many hooks entangled in the vegetation.

Namalee recognized the first mate, a Poonjakee, who
got to his knees and bowed until his head touched a
pile of vegetation. He was overjoyed that the daughter
of Sennertaa had been rescued but distressed that she
should be in such a situation. He eyed Ishmael curiously,
though the fact that the girl regarded Ishmael as a
friend reassured him. But the happiness of the sailors
turned to horror when Namalee, talking so swiftly that
Ishmael could not follow her, told of what had happened to their mother city. Their brown skins turned
gray and they wailed, throwing themselves on the vegetation and beating with their fists. Some pulled out
their bone knives and gashed themselves on the arms
and the chests.

Grief must pay homage, like everything else, to ne-
cessity, which is governed by time. The men ceased
their wailing and applied webs to the wounds. These,
Ishmael was to learn, were woven by a wingless, feath-
erless, fuzzy bird-thing.

While two sailors cut out pieces of the shark's heart,
lungs and liver and removed its stomach, others
searched for the fourth man. After about fifteen minutes,
he was found under a canopy of vines and great leaves.
He had crawled there and died while creepers entered
his wounds and sucked.

The boat in the air was drawn down and Chamkri
and the injured sailor were taken aboard. Namalee and
Ishmael got into the first boat, where they sat on the
thin transparent skin that was both the deck and the
bottom of the hull. They secured themselves with a
fragile-looking but tough skin belt around their waists.
The belt had a buckle of bone and its other ends were
sewn into the deck-skin.

The first mate ordered that more meat be fed to the

amorphous russet and pale green lump of flesh attached to the neck of each of the six bladders secured around the periphery of the boat. Presently the boat began to rise as the bladders swelled. Both vessels unfurled their side sails and, later, the undermast and its boom were lowered through the central shaft in the deck. The shaft was of hollow bone and was the center of twelve spokes which ran to the sides of the boat, where they were connected to the rim of bone which gave the boat its elongated oval shape. The mast was secured to the shaft with a bone pin, and the boom was lowered. Then the sail of the undermast was pulled up to catch the wind.

Some boats, as he was to find out, also had an upper fore-and-aft rigged mast, though this was always shorter and carried less sail than the undermast.

The ascent to the ship took two hours and several more feedings of the gas-generating animals attached to the bladders. Ishmael sat patiently, having mastered the art of waiting during his whaling voyages. Evidently, the sea of the air demanded even more acceptance of the demands of time.

At last, the boats approached the ship at the same altitude and on a parallel course. Lines were thrown from the boat to the ship, where sailors stood inside an enclosure of bone with three sides and a deck. These sailors were tied to the bone beams by lines around their waists so that they would not be pulled out into the air if a gust of wind or an air pocket jerked the boat outward or vertically.

The sails of the boats were furled; the masts and booms were pulled up, telescoped and folded and then locked tightly on the top and bottom of the hull. The boats were then drawn into the enclosures and tied down.

Ishmael found himself inside a long open corridor

which was the main walkway. There were catwalks and ladders running up and down and horizontally and at angles all through the vessel. All were made of hard but hollow and thin-walled bones, most of which came from various species of the wind whales. The great gas bladders were secured in the upper part of the ship in two long rows of ten each. At the base of each was a round broad-mouthed beast.

Ishmael had expected the ship to be covered entirely with skin. But it was a skeleton of a ship with patches of skin here and there, most notably on the bow and aft. The central part was the most open, and this was so because the wind must not be barred from going through to push against the sails on the leeward side. Your ship of the water has no need to consider such a design, since the masts are sticking above the surface and exposed on every side to the wind. But the ship of the air had to be as drafty as possible to sail close-hauled and at the same time permit the wind to push against the square-rigged sails on both port and starboard.

Individual cabins, the galley, some storage spaces, and a few other places were wholly or partially enclosed by skin. But elsewhere the wind, hot or cold, soft or savage, blew on the sailors night and day.

The bridge, or quarterdeck, was situated on the top of the vessel, aft, in a cockpit about two-thirds of the distance back from the bow. Here one steersman handled the wheel, the muscle to move the rudder being provided by headless, footless creatures whose sinews were grown to the end of lines of leather. These had been conditioned to respond to the tuggings and relaxations of lines attached at one end to their muscles and at the other to the shaft of the wheel.

The captain, Baramha, was a tall man on whose forehead was tattooed the symbol of his position: a black ship's wheel crested by a scarlet three-pointed crown. His orders were transmitted by voice to those near him, by signals of hands in the daytime and by lanterns, cages of huge firefly-like insects, at night.

Baramha, hearing Namalee's tale, turned gray and wept and wailed and gashed his chest with a stone knife. After this, he placed himself at the disposal of Namalee. She questioned him about the supply of water and food and *shahamchiz*, a fiery liquor. He assured her that there was enough for them to sail to Zalarapamtra, though the last seven days would find them on short rations. They had killed ten whales so far and stored flesh and water from the carcasses. And they had found in one of them a large *vrishkaw*. This, apparently, was the main reason for the hunting of the leviathans. Ishmael did not know what a *vrishkaw* was, but he determined to find out at the first chance.

The ship put about and sailed close-hauled to keep it in the general direction of the city, which lay to the northwest.

Namalee and Ishmael were conducted to the captain's cabin. This was on the bottom of the hull, directly below the bridge. Since the floor was transparent, Ishmael got an unhindered view of the world thousands of feet below. It also gave him a feeling of anxiety to be standing on such a seemingly frail floor. The skin sagged under each placing of his foot, and it was with relief that he sat on a bone chair which was firmly attached to a bone beam. The cabin was small but open at one end, privacy evidently not being desired by Zalarapamtrans. There was a many-angled desk of reddish bone with a small flat surface on which the captain made his navigational computations or wrote in his log. The log itself was a large book with thin, vellum-like pages on which were large characters in a black ink. The characters looked like no writing that Ishmael had ever seen.

Namalee seated herself while a cabin boy served the first cooked meal the two had eaten for a long time. The whale meat was strange but delicious; the familiar cockroach meat was well steamed and served with a delicious brown-red sauce; and there were piles of a rice-like grain, pale blue, on which a dark orange gravy was poured. The drink was served in skin vessels which had to be lifted up and tilted, the dark green fiery stuff jetting out into their mouths.

Ishmael found himself very comfortable, indeed, almost happy, within a short time. He also found that he was not as fluent talking with the captain as he had been with Namalee. He resolved to cut down on the quantity of *shahamchiz* the next time.

Neither the captain nor Namalee seemed to be affected by the liquor. They continued to pour down great drafts, though their large green eyes did glow as if fires had been lit behind them. Presently, the dishes being taken away, more skins of *shahamchiz* were brought in. Ishmael spoke to Namalee, who looked sharply at him. The captain seemed angered, and then Namalee suddenly smiled and explained that he was not aware of the protocol which he must observe now that they were on a part of Zalarapamtra.

Nevertheless, Ishmael was led away by the boy, who took him up several ladders to a small open-walled cubicle, where he was expected to sleep. He stretched out on his hammock, but he did not sleep at once. The ship did not sail smoothly but lifted and dropped unpredictably. He was glad to be away from the continual slight nausea caused by the never-ending shaking of the earth, but this was almost as bad. The vessel bucked with every updraft or downdraft of air. He would have thought that such a huge structure would sail smoothly on, disdaining the currents that played with lesser things. After a while he slept anyway, and he was to become accustomed to the motion of the vessel. It took him a long time, however, to get used to the transparent fragility on which he walked.

The third day, the first rain clouds he had seen since his arrival darkened the west. An hour later, a wind struck. It was a hard blow but not a typhoon, and the captain had ordered most of the sails furled before the wind reached them. The great ship rolled twenty-five degrees at the first impact and continued to sail leaning to the starboard. Ishmael had strapped himself to the pole of the bottom mat, which extended deep into the vessel. The captain had so ordered, and Ishmael could not understand at first why this particular place was his post. After a while he reasoned that, since he was useless as a hand, he was placed where his weight would give the most stability. He was at least useful as ballast.

The wind became stronger. The ship continued to sail close-hauled but it was being carried eastward off its course. And the wind, now close to typhoon strength, did not blow steadily. It came in gust after gust, as if some mammoth animal over the horizon were blowing, stopping to draw in breath and blowing again. Then rain struck, and lightning and thunder flashed and bellowed somewhere in the clouds.

The captain now had nothing to guide him. He did not possess a compass, since compasses were made of metal, and metal seemed to be absent or at least extremely rare in this world. It might be, Ishmael reasoned, that man had used up the earth's metals. He was well on his way even in the 1840's, if the extrapolations of some scientists could be trusted. How many millions of years had man survived without metals?

That question did not matter. The fact was that the

captain did not even have a lodestone. By day he navigated by the sun and the moon and at night by the stars and the moon. When visibility was cut off, he sailed blindly. He had nothing but the direction of the wind to guide him in this almost complete darkness; if the wind shifted, he would not know which way he was going.

Ishmael sat miserably for an unaccountable time. There were neither watches nor sand glasses in this world nor, for all he knew, even sundials. The human beings living in the days of the end of Time did not seem to care about time.

Occasionally he was replaced, and he slept as well as he could or ate in the galley. He saw no one except a few sailors and the cook. The galley was a cage of bonework. The stove was a securely fixed box of some fire-resistant wood, the heaviest object per cubic inch of anything aboard. The fuel was an oil, not derived from the wind whales, as he had expected, but from a free-floating plant.

Ishmael would have liked to have talked with Cookie for a long time and to study his character, as he did with everybody he met. But the man spoke little and shivered frequently, whenever the ship rolled too far or dropped or rose with shocking suddenness.

Ishmael returned to his seat in the "hold" and sat in a half-drowse most of the time, awakened now and then by the pitching and tossing. Three times, he was sure that the vessel, the *Roolanga*, had been completely swung around several times. If this was so, then the captain was sailing in the opposite direction, unless luck had turned the ship back to its original heading after the whirlings.

He was surprised when the storm suddenly ceased and the clouds began to break away. The red sun was at its zenith, having gone through it twice since the first wind struck. Ishmael had not seen it once during that time; he was taking a sailor's word for it.

The *Roolanga* was headed northwest, but either the wind had carried it straight eastward or it had sailed southeast once or twice after the uncontrollable turnings. Captain Baramha announced that they were off course, which was a way of saying that they were lost. Not until near the end of the day did he know where they were.

To their starboard rose a solid range of mountains that seemed to go up and up until they merged with the dark skies. They were reddish, grayish and blackish and much carved by winds.

Ishmael, lunching with the captain and Namalee, asked how high they went.

Baramha, who had just looked at the primitive altimeter of wood and water, said, "The *Roolanga* is ten thousand feet high. The top of these mountains must be at least four miles up or about twenty-one thousand feet from our altitude. I could take the *Roolanga* up to near the top, but the air would be too thin to breathe."

And so, thought Ishmael, *the Earth had been losing its atmosphere for a billion years.* The plateaus on top of those mountains must once have been the surface of a continent, probably South America. And there would be mountains on top of this mountain, the Andes. How high did they tower? Up where there was no air at all? Or did the Andes exist any more? Or was this South America? Had not some wild-eyed, shockheaded scholar once said that continents, like beans on a thin soup, drifted?

He looked at the terrible cliffs, and a piece fell off with a majestic shrug and a roar that reached him many seconds later. Slowly, perhaps not so slowly, considering the unending shaking, everything high was being brought down.

63

Captain Baramha had laid out a vellum map and indicated where Zalarapamtra was. Ishmael thought that it was on the intermediate plateau of a mountainside that had once been the submerged slope of one of the Samoas. The area to the right of the ship was marked EDGE OF THE WORLD.

From time to time, as he drank more *shahamchiz*, Ishmael looked down through the floor. The long furious rains had swollen the dead seas so that they had drowned their near shores and in many places had joined other seas. Where he had first landed, he would now find water and would have to dive a dozen feet or more to reach the roof of the jungle.

One of the seas they passed during that long lunch was red, and Ishmael, asking about it, was told that the red air brit had been forced down into the water by the rains.

"Does that explain why I have seen no clouds of brit?" he said.

"Yes," the captain said. "The rains are vitally needed, and they must come, or else all life dies. But they also bring some bad, as every good does. They wash out the brit, and it takes many days before the breeding grounds to the west can produce new. During this time, the great wind whales go hungry and get lean. And the smaller life which feeds on the brit also starves. And the sharks and other predators find that they can eat more of the weakened browsers. They stuff themselves and grow fat, and it is then that the sharks breed. But their eggs, which they produce by the billions, and which float in clouds like the brit, are eaten by the whales. Only a few of the eggs hatch. So I can also say that the bad brings some good with it.

"After a while, the seeds of the great plants that grow far to the west, at the base of the cliffs there"—*Africa?* Ishmael thought, *India? Indo-China?*—"explode and send the brit high. And the whales begin to eat that, and the sharks eat the smaller creatures and occasionally a sick or wounded whale, and everything is restored as it was before the rains came."

The conversation turned to other matters, including Ishmael's story of the world from which he had come and what had happened after he had met Namalee. Ishmael understood after a while that Namalee had said nothing of the times when he had touched her or they kept each other warm. She must not have been exaggerating when she had said that her people would kill him if he molested a "vestal virgin." By molesting, of course, she meant even an accidental touch.

After the lunch, the captain said that they must all give thanks to the little god of the *Roolanga*, Ishnuvakardi, who would in turn pass on their thanks and his, the little god's, to the great god, Zoomashmarta. They arose and climbed down a ladder to the central walkway and thence forward to a room walled in transparent skin but painted with religious scenes and symbols.

On an altar of bone was a bone box. Namalee took her place before it, donning a headdress of bone on which hundreds of the tiny red brit had been glued. A tiny fire burned in a wooden cup before the box.

All of the crew except those on duty were there. They fell to their knees when Namalee turned to them, intoning something in a language that was not the one she had taught Ishmael. He dropped to his knees too, because he felt that the others expected it. There was no reason to be stiff-necked or even discourteous. Nor was this the first time he had made obeisance to unChristian gods, he thought. There was Hypocrisy and Greed and Hate and a pantheon of other deities of civilization. And he had taken part in the worship of Queequeg's idol, Yojo, with no afterqualms at all.

He got to his knees before the altar and the box, reflecting as the floor skin sagged under his weight and he looked down through thousands of feet of air, that he had never been so close to eternity before in a temple.

Namalee turned, still chanting, and lifted the box up. It had hidden an image about a foot high, carved of some ivory-white substance striated with red, green and black. It was half-whale and half-human, combining a bestial face with a human torso to the waist and a wind whale's tail where the legs should have been. It radiated an odor that was sweet and pleasant and, he was certain, intoxicating.

He had drunk enough *shahamchiz* to make him reel a little when he walked. But on sniffing the odor of the idol, he felt his senses staggering and after a while he fell flat on his face. Within a few seconds, he had passed out.

He awoke on the floor looking through several miles of air at the half-dead seas beneath. When he managed to sit up, groaning, he found that he was alone. His head ached as if he had been hit with a hammer. Or as if the Urfather of all hangovers had visited him just to show what gigantic aches the head of Adam had endured.

The box was over the idol. The remnants of the sweet and drunk-making odor were still in the room.

He staggered back to his cubicle and lay down and went to sleep.

When he awoke, he intended to ask about the perfume and its effects, but he found everybody too busy to talk to him. All the scurrying about and the transmission of orders was caused by the sighting of a pod of wind whales. The captain had decided that they must pause in their return homeward to hunt for food.

Otherwise they would starve before they got near Zalarapamtra.

Ishmael felt much improved and, though his discre-
tion told him that he was foolish, he asked the captain
if he could take part in the hunt. He listed his qualifi-
cations, most of which consisted of a long and intense
experience in hunting the monsters of the sea. But he
could not see why he could not adapt himself to the
requirements of the air.

"We could use an extra hand," Captain Baramha said.
"But we can't have any clumsy or ignorant persons
interfering at a critical moment. However, you do know
how to sail, and the main difference between your experience and that of my crew is that you will be
sailing in three dimensions instead of two. Very well.
You will go with Karkri's boat. Go there at once and
get your instructions."

The crew of an air ship never carried more than two
extra hands because of weight restrictions. The *Roolanga* had lost one man early in its voyage when he
had leaped or fallen off the ship while on night watch.
Then Rashvarpa had died when thrown out of the
boat, and a companion had broken his bones. So, need-
ing all the help he could get, even if it was inexpert,
the captain had accepted Ishmael.

Karkri, the harpooner, was not of the stature or mus-
culature of the savage harpooners, men like lions, that
Ishmael had known. No Daggoos, Tashtegos or Quee-
quegs, these men were short and slight. Their legs were
thin but their shoulders and arms were well developed.
It did not take powerful muscles to drive a shaft into
the head of a wind whale, if a man knew where to
cast. There were many large openings in the skull under the thin tissue wrapping it. At the last moment
the harpooner had to stand in the bow of the bucking
boat as it ran alongside the monster and, hooking his

feet under leather straps secured to the skin of the bottom of the boat, throw his lance. If it went through one of the wide gaps in the fragile and hollow structure, it would drive into the brain, the heart or the lungs. These organs were located inside the head, the kidneys, liver, spleen and others being strung out along the largely hollow interior of the whale's body. The whale, if stripped of his skin, would be revealed as mostly air and bladders enclosed in the bones. Ishmael, thinking of this and wondering if there was enough meat on the leviathan to justify the dangerous hunt, got into Karkri's boat. The harpooner looked dubious but said nothing. A sailor, Koojai, told Ishmael what he had to do. Ishmael had talked to some of the crew about the boats before the great storm and so knew the theory of sailing an air boat.

Once the four were strapped in, the boat was pushed out at the ends of long poles from its nest in the side of the ship. It drifted outward and was quickly left behind.

The two masts, one on top and one on the bottom, were swiveled to the horizontal by a joint near the butt and locked in place. The masts and yardarms were very slim and very light sections of bones fitting tightly into one another. After the boat was cast loose the crewmen rose, crouching. One reached down through a hole in the bottom of the hull, which was only a thin transparent skin, and unlocked the joint. Then, pulling on lines, they straightened the mast out and relocked it at the joint. The yardarm of the fore-and-aft rig was unlocked, straightened properly and relocked.

The upper mast was shorter and its sail smaller to ensure that it was more than counterbalanced by the mast beneath. After it was raised, the sail of the undermast was unfurled by lines attached to it. There were many small holes on the skin of the bottom so that a sailor could reach through to do his work. These had to be watched for when a crewman walked around the boat, but there was little walking once the sails were set.

Karkri had unfolded the enormous rudders, horizontal and vertical, used to steer the ship. He gave it over to the steersman and crawled as close to the central part of the boat as he could. In this light vessel, balance was important, and every shift of weight had to be carefully performed.

The sails caught the wind, and the boat forged swiftly ahead, overtaking the enormous mother ship even though it was departing at an angle from it. Ishmael, as the green hand, tended to the care of the upper sail. Koojai watched the other sail through the clear skin of the boat, ready to pull or release lines as ordered. If Koojai failed to receive an order because the harpooner was too busy or incapacitated, Koojai would carry out the operation on his own. It was also necessary for him to keep an eye on the inexperienced man and to make sure that he carried out his functions at the same time. It would never do to swing the upper boom one way and the lower another.

Karkri, having secured himself in the seat at the bow, then told his crew that they were out for air sharks, too.

"We need meat, men. Meat to feed us and the bladder-creatures. Even if we killed every one of the thirty giants in the pod ahead of us, we still would not have enough. So when the sharks come nosing around to tear at our quarry, we will tear at them."

The boat passed the ship. Ishmael saw Namalee standing on a catwalk on the starboard side, and he smiled at her. She smiled back and then she disappeared.

Ishmael saw that the bow of the ship was now opened and asked Koojai about it.

"When the ship enters the brit-cloud, it will act like a wind whale," Koojai said. "The tiny creatures will billow into the funnel-like opening, and they will be caught in nets and reaped. They are hard on the teeth if a man tries to crunch them raw, but cooked they become soft. They make a very nutritious and passably palatable soup."

There were four other boats out. One was teamed with Karkri's, and it sailed about a quarter of a mile to the north on a parallel course with his. The common quarry was a leviathan the color of a ripe plum. Koojai said that it was a bull, and it was the rear sentinel of the pod. It rolled from side to side and traced an invisible wiggly line on the horizontal plane as it tried to keep all four boats in its sight. Then it was within the red cloud, and a moment later Ishmael's boat plunged after it. But the crew had placed goggles over their eyes and wrapped thin skins around their mouths.

Thousands of tiny parachute shapes, each about the size of a pumpkin seed, pelted Ishmael. They broke up against the hard skin of his goggles and smeared them with red. He had to keep wiping away at them to see anything, though there was nothing to see even when they were clean.

The impacts felt as if enormous hands were gently patting him all over his body. He turned his head away and saw that Koojai had slipped off his mouth-protection for a moment. He collected a mouthful of the red creatures and then replaced the mask. After he had chewed gently for a minute, red juice trickled from the corners of his lips.

Presently Karkri ordered that everybody should scoop out with one hand the piles of tiny bodies collecting on the bottom of the boat. Ishmael, keeping one hand free for handling the lines, scraped up handful after handful and cast them to one side. But others fell in a reddish snowstorm and piled up, and the boat became sluggish.

There were spaces within the cloud free of the brit, however, for some reason of which no one had informed Ishmael. The illumination within was like twilight, and the monster ahead had become quite black. There was also less wind, and the sails did not belly out so fully. This loss of speed was matched by that of the whales, who had gained weight while going through the cloud. They had taken on great cargos of the brit, which were being distributed through the stomachs looped like spaghetti strings along the bones of the tail.

Ishmael dipped his hand again and again until the brit, like seeds, had been scattered outward. By then the two boats were about two hundred feet apart and about three hundred feet behind the great tail-fins. There they stayed, unable to catch up with the beast, and then they dived into the semisolid cloud again.

Once more they emerged into a cleared space, as if coming from a forest into a meadow. This time they found themselves between two of the monsters, the second meal having slowed most of the pod. And, after being bailed out again, the boats increased their speed. Soon Ishmael's was even with the whale's head and drawing up to the eye, red as the heart of a forge, big and round as a factory chimney, yet seeming small in the Brobdingnagian skull.

The beast rolled forty-five degrees each way on its axis, striving to learn if there were other hunters below or above it. Then it steadied and sailed on, though it could have evaded its pursuers by discharging a ballast of water or loosing gas. It would not if it followed the age-old ways of its ancestors; a whale never seemed to learn that a lance would fly out for the hole in the skull about ten feet back of the eye.

Karkri stood up, his feet shoved under straps on the

floor. He raised his goggles and he checked again the coiling of the line around the fore post. Then he raised his free hand, the other holding the long thin bone shaft with the long thin bone head, and he made a short chopping movement.

Koojai stood up also. He twisted the end of a short stick of polished brown wood and then hurled it into the air straight up. It turned over and over, high above the upper mast, high above the head of the beast. Almost at the same time, a similar stick appeared on the other side of the head. Both exploded at one end. Smoke curled out in streamers that described circles as the sticks, still rotating, began to fall.

The twisting of one end had broken off a chemical which flowed into another and set off a generation of gas. This ruptured the thin end and, with the inrush of air, the chemicals began to burn.

The sticks were the signals that the boats were ready. Whoever threw the first stick waited until the second gave its signal before taking action.

Karkri balanced himself, rocking a little, the floor giving way to each shift of weight and the boat also rocking. Then he hurled the lance and the line, thin almost to the point of invisibility, followed. The shaft tore through the skin of the beast and disappeared.

Karkri had sunk to one knee after the throw. Now he fell back and grabbed the strap and buckled its wooden tongue to hold him fast to the bow position. The line whirled off a spindle as the beast loosed from its underside several tons of silvery water. It rose swiftly, rotating its wing-sails so that they would present the least surface to the air during its ascent.

Ishmael had but one chance to look at the leviathan, and then he was busy furling the sail. Koojai worked to draw up the sail of the undermast. The rudderman waited for the jerk that would either snatch the craft upward or break the line.

Karkri waited with his bone knife in hand. He could do nothing now but hang on until the beast got tired, but he must be alert for the situation that would require cutting of the line.

Ishmael tied up the sail and secured the boom. He looked upward. The whale was dwindling, though it was still huge. The other boat was even with them, its crew waiting tensely for the first jerk of the line. The harpooner turned his dark face and flashed white teeth at Karkri.

The line raced outward and upward from the whistling spindle, which leaned forward a little on the hinge at its lowest end. Abruptly, the spindle stopped, and the nose of the boat turned upward, and then the boat was rising. Though the line looked fragile enough for Ishmael to pull it apart with his hands, it held. Together, the two boats soared.

The wind whale was almost two hundred yards above them. Below, the red cloud drifted by. The *Roolanga* was hidden in it for a moment and then it emerged from the western side, beating against the wind. The other boats were a mile to the east and somewhat below, also being dragged upward by a beast.

The wind whistled through the rigging. The air became colder and the sky darker. Their heads grew light, and they had to suck in deep breath. Far below, the *Roolanga* was a stick with wings.

Karkri, despite the weakness caused by the thin air, was winding the spindle with a stick he had inserted through a hole. It was now necessary that the boats be drawn as closely as possible to the animal before he decided to dive. Rising, he could not jerk the line nearly as violently as he would when he loosed the gas from the bladders and upended and fell head-foremost. And so Karkri and the harpooner in the other boat worked as swiftly as they could. And when they could not move an arm, and their breaths came so strongly that it seemed they must burn their throats, they secured the spindle and crawled aft. Ishmael relinquished his post to Karkri and took up the task. Though he was larger and more heavily muscled, he did not last as long as Karkri. If they had been at sea level, where he had spent most of his life, he might have surpassed the little brown man. But here, in the upper reaches to which Karkri was accustomed, Ishmael's breath gave out and his arms felt as if he were convalescing from a long illness.

Koojai, grinning at Ishmael, crawled past him to take his turn. Then the steersman gave up his post to Karkri, and after a while Karkri was working again. Ishmael took his second turn, lasting a shorter time than the first. By the third turn of duty, he felt as if he could not crawl to the bow, let alone turn the spindle, which now seemed to have rusted tight. But he went up the almost vertical slope of the deck, using the holes in it as a ladder, and strapped himself in and strove mightily to make a few turns. He succeeded, locked the spindle, and crawled back. Once he looked back, and he wished that he had not. Where was the *Roolanga*?

The boats had drawn up steadily until they were now about thirty feet behind the gigantic fin-sails. Karkri called a halt then. If the whale dived now, he could not put too sudden a strain on the lines.

Ishmael's heart would not stop pounding, and his breath sawed in and out. The whale was getting dim; was this the prelude to the fuzziness of mind, the sometimes suicidal actions resulting from the drunkenness of the heights? He hoped that the others, who were better able to live in this poverty of atmosphere, would watch over him. Perhaps . . .

He came fully to his senses with the air rushing by and the sky suddenly not quite so dark. The boat was tipped almost vertically downward. The dead sea sparkled in the light of the red sun; the *Roolanga* was directly below and seemed destined to be struck headlong by the beast.

Indeed, this had happened before, though never, according to the sailors, by design. The whale sometimes miscalculated its vectors and struck a ship. And when that happened the ship was lucky to stay in one piece.

They shot within fifty feet of the *Roolanga*. Ishmael saw the men staring out at them from behind the transparent skin and in the open spaces. Some heads were also sticking up out of cockpits on the upper deck, or top, of the vessel. Some waved; others joined their hands together and bowed forward, praying to the lesser god of the ship and to Zoomashmarta that this dive end safely for their fellows.

Though several minutes must have passed, they seemed seconds. The earth spread outward; the shores of the sea shot away; and then there was nothing but water below.

Ishmael remembered how the whale had so successfully smacked the boat against the earth when he and Namalee watched. That happened seldom, the sailors had said. But it did happen.

Usually the whale ended the dive and began rising with plenty of room to spare for the boats swinging behind it. Say, twenty feet or so. Yes, it was scary. Even the oldest hand became frightened when this happened, unless you were talking of Old Bharanhi.

Old Bharanhi was the Paul Bunyan of the sailors of the air, and he was never frightened. He had lived long ago, when men were giants, and . . .

With an explosion, the giant wing-sails snapped out from the beast's side, where they had been tightly folded. The starboard wing narrowly missed striking the harpoon line. The whale checked its speed, and the boat gained on it. There was nothing for Karkri to do. To have tried to haul in even more line would have meant being caught in the middle of a turn, and the unlocked spindle would run out the whole length of line. The length of the arc the boat would then describe as the whale turned upward would be deadly.

Ishmael understood now why that first boat had crashed. The crew had not been able to haul up the boat to the animal as closely as they wished.

Koojai, behind him, shrieked something. Perhaps it was a prayer, though it was considered bad form to say anything beyond what duty required, and then the forward part of the boat was snapped upward with a force that drove Ishmael's thighs against the strap and sent a pain shooting across his back.

The sea charged them and then suddenly sprang aside. They were in the sky; then they were swinging back toward the sea.

On the second swing, Ishmael saw why Koojai had cried out.

The other whale, also coming up out of the dive, was heading for them.

Apparently it saw that they were going to collide, for it rotated its wings to present a fully resistant surface to the air. It slowed and dipped, but not quite enough. Its head struck the other whale just back of its head, and the skin and the fragile bone of Ishmael's whale crumpled under the impact.

The head also rammed into the line, jerking the boat and snapping the line.

Ishmael was catapulted forward, saw the plum-colored skin expand out before him, hit it head-first, went through it like an arrow, struck a number of things—organs and bones, probably—was turned on his back, while still falling, and went through the skin on the other side or the underpart. He could never be sure. He was half-conscious and half-aware that he was falling. The two behemoths were blurs above him; another and smaller blur might have been one of the boats.

He did not remember striking the water, and that he did awake testified that he had fallen in feet-first and straight up. He was choking with the saltiness in his throat and nose, and he was fighting to get his head above the surface.

Then his head cleared the heavy liquid, and a hundred yards away he saw something he never expected to see again, though he would never forget it. The black coffin floated on top of the water as if it were on the Styx and carrying Queequeg slowly, dawdling with the certainty that time did not count now, toward the other shore.

A shadow flashed by. Beyond the coffin-canoe, by several hundred yards, the two whales, one entangled in the entrails of the other, crashed.

The coffin lifted with the first wave, rolled, turned and headed toward him.

He looked for the two boats and their crews. One boat was lying bent in half on the surface about a hundred yards away. Its flatness showed that the gas bladders had been broken, but one mast, minus a boom, projected drunkenly.

He counted three heads of swimmers and several still floaters.

Above, while tacking, two boats were sinking toward them.

The coffin rushed bow-first at him. He reached up and gripped the carvings, as he had done after the sinking of the *Pequod*, and hauled himself onto it. The odor of pitch was still strong. After all, it had not been long, in terms of the days of his life, since the carpenter had nailed shut the lid and caulked the seams.

A man swimming toward him suddenly threw up his arms, screamed, and went down under the surface.

It was evident that he had not dived. And even if, for instance, he had suffered a heart attack, he was not going to sink. He would have floated.

Something had pulled him under. After a few minutes, Ishmael knew that it was keeping the man under.

Up until then, Ishmael had taken it for granted that the seas were empty of life. He still could not believe that any fish existed in this poisonously salty element. The predator must be an air-breather.

Ishmael shouted at the other men, telling them what had happened. They began to pull themselves toward the shore, and he began to paddle the coffin-buoy. As he did so, he felt a tingling in the hands, born of his fear that something would tear off a hand as it dipped into the water.

But no such thing happened, and the other swimmers reached the shore unhurt. They helped Ishmael pull the buoy up on the quaking shore and then they gazed out over the sea. The bodies of the floaters had disappeared. Whatever it was that had seized the swimmer had also disposed of the corpses. Ishmael asked the sailors if they knew what prowled under the heavy sullen surfaces, and they replied that they knew nothing of the dead seas. They had never seen, or heard of, any life in them. But then they were inhabitants of the air, and they entered the dead seas only by accident.

"But leave by permission of an unseen host," Ishmael said, shivering.

The two air boats drifted in, sails furled, undermasts folded, and threw out lines which the men grabbed. They pulled the boats down and climbed aboard. Ishmael, looking back down at Queequeg's coffin, longed for it because it was his only link to home, the planet orbiting about the sun of dead Time. It also might be the only key to return, since, if a man could go ahead of time in Time, why not backtrack in Time? And it could be that the mysterious schematics carved on the lid of the coffin were in some as-yet-incomprehensible manner keys to be twisted against the tumblers of Time.

On board the ship, he requested permission to be admitted to the captain. There he asked that a boat be sent back to pick up the coffin. At first Captain Baramha was outraged at the expenditure of time and energy if this were done. But Namalee overruled his denial, and Baramha accepted her ruling without apparent resentment. This was because she said that the coffin was a religious matter, and in religion she had the final word. Ishmael did not follow her reasoning, unless she thought that the coffin was his god, but he did not ask her to clarify. He was content to have the deed; the explanation could wait.

Two boats went down, and the coffin was taken aboard and lashed down, one half supported on one boat and the other half on the second boat. The two crafts had been tied together for greater buoyancy and each had only two crewmen. Then the double-craft arose slowly, the mouth-creatures of the bladders eating triple portions of food to generate gas. Eventually, while the captain strode back and forth on his bridge, his lips moving soundlessly, the boats were drawn into the ports of the ship. The coffin was tied down in the center of gravity of the ship, and the boatmen went to work to help cut up and store the two whales that had been killed.

Later the boats went out again, this time drawing pieces of meat behind them on bladders. When the air sharks came in for passes at the bait, they were harpooned. Those not killed at once followed the same rising and diving tactics as the whales, but they lacked the gas-generating capabilities or the weight of the leviathans.

After a dozen sharks were killed, the ship resumed sailing. But it still lacked enough meat, so the first time it encountered another cloud of atmospheric brit, it hunted again. It was not until near the end of the long day that there was enough meat aboard to supply them until they reached Zalarapamtra.

The last whale killed gave up to the cutting butchers a prize that would have been the cause of a great celebration at any other time.

It was a round ivory-hard substance two feet in diameter, alternately striated with red, blue and black. It exuded a powerful perfume that caused drunkenness in those who came near. This was the same perfume that the little god of the ship, Ishnuvakardi, exuded.

The ball was found in one of the smaller stomachs of the whale, the creature having many stomachs distributed along the bony framework of the tail. Namalee said that a certain small creature of the air, a *vrishwanka*, was sometimes swallowed by a whale. It passed through the entrails that climbed around the skeleton of the tail until it was either eliminated or caught in a blind corner of a sac. If the latter happened, the digestive system of the whale secreted a substance around the *vrishwanka* just as an oyster did around a grain of sand.

The result, the intoxicatingly perfumed, ivory-hard *vrishkaw*, was a great treasure. Out of it would be carved a new little god, and the god would be put in a newly carved temple in the city of Zalarapamtra. Sometimes the uncarved *vrishkaw* was traded to a city with which Zalarapamtra did not happen to be warring at that time. The other city may have lost a god when a ship went down and needed a new one. Or the god may have been traded for by one of those cities that hoarded gods against the day when a shortage would occur. Or hoarded because of the belief that the more gods, the more good fortune.

Namalee, during one of their many talks during the long, long journey back, told him of how the gods of Zalarapamtra were found and "born," as she called the process of carving.

She also told him of how, when old whales died, their flesh fed their own bladders, and they rose upward where the sky became totally black in the daytime and there was little air. The mighty corpses drifted with the high winds eastward and then began to sink as, one after the other, the bladders burst from corruption. And somewhere at the foot of the insurmountable mountains to the east (which Ishmael knew were the once submarine slopes of continents) was a place where the dead whales ended up. There was a tangle of bones almost as high as the cliffs, since the beasts had been drifting there since time began. And there, of course, was an immense treasure of *vrishkaw*, of perfume-exuding unborn gods.

The city that found the ancient burial grounds of the wind whales would be the richest in the world and hence the most powerful.

And also the drunkenest, Ishmael thought. He envisioned a city thronged with such gods, the citizens reeling during waking hours, falling soddenly into bed, rising as intoxicated as when they went to bed.

Many a ship from many a city had put out with the sole purpose of locating the burial ground, Namalee said. But it was near the eastern cliffs that the Purple Beasts of the Stinging Death were most numerous.

"How do you know that?" Ishmael said.

"Because none of the ships that look for the burial

ground ever come back," she said. "Obviously they were caught by a Purple Beast."

He raised his eyebrows and smiled.

She said, "What are you thinking?"

"That, strange as you and your people are to my way of thinking, you are still much like me and my people. The essential human has not changed. Whether that is good or not, I cannot say. Indeed, I cannot say that there is any good or evil beyond what each person thinks is beneficial or not to himself. When I think of the billions upon billions, the trillions upon trillions, who have lived and struggled for or against evil, which has been called many names but always wears a skull, then I wonder."

What the white whale had been to Ahab, time was to Ishmael.

The red sun finally went down, and the slowly chilling night came. Days and nights followed, though not swiftly. Ishmael learned everything there was to learn about sailing and navigating a ship of the air and also much about building one. He was a forecastle hand, yet he sometimes ate with the captain and Namalee. That he was clearly of a different race, of a totally unknown race, and that he claimed to be the son of a different sun and a different world, raised him above class distinctions.

There was also the possibility that they thought him insane, though quite capable in many respects. They delighted to hear him talk of his own world, but they could not comprehend much of what he said. When they heard him say that the very air through which they sailed, so many thousands of feet above the ground, had once been filled with water, and that this water was filled with life unlike that which they knew, they could not believe him.

Equally incredible was his insistence that the earth

he had known shook only now and then and quite briefly.

Ishmael did not argue with them any more than he would have with Ahab. Each man's mind was cast into its own coinage, and each could be spent as currency only in a small kingdom.

As the *Roolanga* neared Zalarapamtra, its crew became silent. The sailors talked, but only in very low tones, and they said little most of the time. They seemed lost in themselves, as if they were searching in their own minds for what they would do if they indeed did find their native country desolated. They went frequently into the chapel, as Ishmael called it, where Namalee was spending most of her waking and many of her sleeping hours. The box was off the little god all the time now, and Ishmael could not go by the open room without feeling his senses stumble.

Namalee sat on the floor, facing the god, with her body leaning forward almost parallel to the floor and her head bent almost touching the floor. Her long black hair was thrown forward so that it spread out like a cloud of incense.

Then the top of a mountain leaned out over the northwest horizon, and the captain called everybody to his post. They sailed all that day and into the night and when the red sun reluctantly came up again, they were overshadowed by the colossus. Dead ahead was a tremendous shelf of stone, and on the stone was the city of Zalarapamtra.

A cry arose from the ship.

The shelf was a jumble of rocks and debris.

Ishmael had asked Namalee how men could live in stone chambers that shook and trembled and threatened to come down on their heads every instant.

The answer was that few *lived* in the stone chambers. These were used for storage, for retreat from storms or enemies, and as places of worship they constituted the lower half of the city. The upper part was, in essence, a floating city. It consisted of two levels of hundreds of houses and larger buildings attached together and buoyed by thousands of great gas-bladders. The floating residential half was anchored at many places to the surface of the shelf, and passage between the floating city and the stone city was by means of ladders or flexible stairways.

All of this had been destroyed. Something had broken the bladders and exploded and burned the upper levels. Their charred and shattered remains were strewn and piled over the stone part. And this had been blasted open at many places to expose the chambers beneath. Piles of fragmented rock lay everywhere.

The *Roolanga* sailed back and forth before the tremendous shelf and several times over it before the captain decided to bring it into a dock. This was a sunken place carved into the lip of the shelf. The ship floated in with sails furled and the masts shipped. Sailors leaped off of the vessel as it slid into the rectangular depression, and they seized lines thrown them by those on the ship. The lines were run through carved stone rings projecting from the walls of the dock, looped through and then tightened. The ship slowed down even more and came to rest with the tip of its bow only a few inches from the rear wall of the dock. More gas was released from the great bladders, and the ship settled down until its keel almost touched the floor of the pier.

Half of the crew of thirty stayed aboard; the other half went into the ruins.

The shelf had its roots in an immense canyon, a slash in the body of the mountain. This rose so high that its top was a thread of dark blue. The massive shelf projected out into the air for perhaps half a mile, so that a shaft sunk through it would have ended in air and a view of the detritus-strewn slope beneath. Ishmael wondered that men would build on a ledge that was doomed to break off from the never-ending vibrations. But Namalee said that even if the stone did fall, it would snap off the anchors when it fell, and the two floating levels would remain in the air. That was the theory at least.

Water was provided most of the year by a spring at the base of the innermost wall of the canyon and the rest of the year by pods harvested from the vegetation at the foot of the mountain.

Ishmael thanked her for the information. He then asked her why she had been delegated to lead this party, when it would have been wiser to leave the only woman survivor, as far as anyone knew, on board. She replied that the members of the family of the Grand Admiral had many privileges which lesser beings did not have. To pay for these, they also had more obligations. Until a male member of her family was found, she was the leader and she must be at the head of any perilous undertaking.

Ishmael did not understand the reasoning behind this. If Zalarapamtra was to live again, it must have woman to bear children.

They climbed piles of stone and burned wood, skirted deep jagged holes and sometimes leaped over the holes. The blasts had ripped off the floor at many places, exposing the chambers beneath. These were partially filled with stone rubble or with the remains of the upper city.

Nowhere was there even a single bone.

"The Beast eats everything, flesh, bones, everything," Namalee said. "It settles down over the city after it has ruined it, and its stinging tentacles probe into every place and sting those who still live. And it drags out the dead into its mouth. When it has eaten everything, it sleeps. And then it floats off, looking for other prey.

"It has destroyed three cities during my lifetime: Avastshi, Prakhamarshri, and Manvrikaspa. It comes, and it kills, and it leaves few alive behind."

"But it does leave *some?*" Ishmael said.

He noted great streaks of some dirty white substance and wondered if the Beast left a slime.

"Avastshi and Manvrikaspa were emptied of all life," she said. "A woman and two of her babies escaped in Prakhamashri because the entrance to the chamber in which she was hiding was blocked by rubble."

"And did these cities come to life again when the whaling ships returned?" Ishmael said.

"Only Prakhamashri thrives today," she said. "Whalers of the other two also returned with their daughters of the Grand Admiral. But they were few and one thing and another happened, and presently there were no women alive. So the surviving men boarded their ships and floated away with sails furled while they sniffed in the odors of the little gods and the great god, which they carried in the flagship. Then they hurled the gods overboard into the salty sea and jumped after them and the ships drifted on until they sank against the land."

A national suttee, Ishmael told himself. *If all the states have such customs, it is remarkable that mankind has survived this long. And I get the impression that there is not much of humanity walking around under this red sun.*

The party proceeded slowly toward the canyon while the rocks under their feet quivered. There was nothing but devastation around them and a silence broken only thinly by them. Then they heard a cry, and a moment later a head appeared from a hole in the rock near the mouth of the canyon. Another head popped out, then two more. One woman, one man and two girl children had escaped the Purple Beast of the Stinging Death.

They had also escaped the men of Booragangah, who had come after the Beast had left.

They had returned to the deepest chamber and there the man had swung shut an immense door of stone which he had worked hard for years to shape. They had lived on water and food stored there for just such an emergency. But they had been lucky to get to the room, because the onslaught of the Beast had been unexpected and terrible and seemingly on all points at once.

"And then, almost immediately after it left, the ships of the Booragangah came," the man said. "It was still night, so I slipped out and hid in the rubble and listened. Men of Zalarapamtra! Namalee, daughter of the Grand Admiral! The men of Booragangah boasted that they had lured the Beast here! Their ships had sighted one headed toward their city. Perhaps it would have attacked them and perhaps it would have missed them. One never knows about the *kahamwoodoo*. It floats along as if it were a cloud, and it does not seem to care to do anything but float most of the time. But sometimes it changes its course and heads for a city, and that city is doomed.

"But the Booragangah whalers caught whales and fed them to the *kahamwoodoo*, losing two ships that got too close, though. The *kahamwoodoo* finally turned after them . . ."

"How?" Ishmael said. "I thought the Beast had no wing-sails."

"By a series of small controlled explosions," Namalee said. "It shoots out fire and smoke with much noise from holes in its bodies. The thing that makes the noise and smoke is also the thing it drops on the cities to blow them apart."

"A beast that shoots gunpowder and drops bombs?" Ishmael said. He used the English words for gunpowder and bombs, since these did not exist in Namalee's language.

"It shoots fire, smoke and noise, and drops stones that explode," she said.

"The men of Booragangah said that their Grand Admiral, who was in charge of their great whaling fleet, conceived the idea. His name is Shamvashra. Remember that, citizens of Zalarapamtra! Shamvashra! He is the fiend of the upper air who has destroyed our city!"

Ishmael thought that Shamvashra was only doing what they would have done if they had thought of it, but he said nothing.

"It was necessary, they said, to work harder than they ever had in their lives. They had to keep on slaying whales and launching them toward the Beast. And they lost a ship with all men aboard while they were hunting food for the Beast when one was struck by two whales diving through the brit with the boats attached to them. But the men said that the ships they had lost made a price worth paying, because they had lured the Beast to Zalarapamtra. They said that they might try to do the same with other Beasts for all of their enemies, and then they would fear no other cities, because there would be none.

"Other men said that that would be bad. What if they met a Beast that could not be lured away and it destroyed Booragangah? That would be the end of man.

"But most seemed to be happy about what they had done. So they took our great god, Zoomashmarta, and all the lesser gods, put them aboard their ships and sailed away."

At these words, a cry went up from the sailors and from Namalee; they wept and some gashed themselves.

"No gods!" Namalee cried. "Zalarapamtra is without gods! They are prisoners of Booragangah!"

"We are lost!" a sailor shouted.

The man who was telling the story said, "I heard them say that they would be coming back some day and making sure that we did not build a new great city. They would surprise the people who returned on the ships and would slay them or carry them off as slaves. And this place would know only the air sharks, sweeping above the ruins and eyeing them in vain for life on which to feed."

"We will be powerless without our gods!" another man said.

They found no other survivors. On returning to the ship, the crew spread the news. The captain, informed by Namalee, turned gray and cut himself so deeply in his grief that he came close to dying of loss of blood.

Until they landed, they had all believed that, horrible as the situation was, they would flourish again. After all, they had their gods. Though these might permit disaster to fall upon Zalarapamtra, they would not permit their worshippers to die out. Who then would the gods have to worship them?

They had not considered, of course, that Avastshi and Manvrikaspa had had their gods, and these had permitted their worshippers to die to the last one.

They were a gloomy crew and, what was worse, hopeless. Gloom derived from despair is something that hope can overcome, but hope can only come if something occurs to make things seem not hopeless. Even the arrival in the next three days of five whaling ships did not reassure them. If anything, the addition of more people seemed to add to the despair. The city was almost as silent as when it had held but four people in hiding.

Six more days passed. There was more activity then,

since it was necessary to put to air and hunt for food. Captain Baramha died from infection of his wounds and a lack of desire to live. His ship took him out high above the dead seas and, after a short ceremony, his naked body was slid overboard from a plank.

"You still have the gods of the ships," Ishmael said. "Why can't . . . ?"

"They have power only over the ship," she said. "They are very little gods. No, we must have the gods of the city and the greatest god, Zoomashmarta."

"Otherwise you just all give up and die, is that it?" Ishmael said.

They did not reply, and it was evident from their faces that that was exactly what they would do. They were sitting around a number of fires in an underground chamber which had been repaired. The fires were small and comparatively smokeless. Ventilation was provided by holes in the ceiling, and light by giant fireflies in cages. The room quivered with the earth tide.

Ishmael sat with Namalee and her five sisters and the captains of the ships around one fire. The first mates sat around another, and the second mates around still another. The sailors were in other chambers.

Ishmael wondered how many human beings were alive on the face of this Earth. If they all had such fatalistic attitudes, they would often encounter situations where it would be easier to give up and let death take over. Was this indeed happening everywhere? Had mankind been so long a voyager in time that he had wearied of the journey? Were the slow red sun and the nearing moon constant reminders that the struggle could end in only one way?

Or were the societies of the South Pacific sea bottoms the only ones to have this attitude? Did groups elsewhere have the unceasing drive, the desire to live, that had possessed human beings in Ishmael's day?

Ishmael looked at Namalee and became angry. It was not right that such a beautiful young woman should be surrendering to death just because of some carved pieces of perfumed ivory.

He stood up and spoke loudly. The others, squatting, looked up at him expectantly. Consciously or not, he realized, they had prayed that he, the stranger, would not be bound by their customs and laws and would give them that spark they lacked.

"When you hunt the great wind whale, you are not cowards," Ishmael said. "I know that. No craven gets into a tiny boat and strikes deep into the head of such a monster and then lets that monster drag him so high and so low with death whistling like the wind past his ears every second.

"And I am sure that when it comes to fighting other men, you are as brave."

He paused, looked around, noting that the women were looking directly at him but that the men were looking at the floor.

"But," he said even more loudly, "you need to get your courage from something outside you! You must have your gods if you are to act like men! Your courage is breathed into you from the outside! It does not live within you and breathe on your heart and make it as hot as the coals of those fires!"

"It is the gods who control this world!" Namalee said. "What can we do without them?"

Ishmael paused. What indeed could they do? Nothing, unless he did something for them first. And he had been so accustomed to the spectator's part, or to a minor role, that he now found it strange and frightening to be the prime mover, the chief actor.

"What can you do without the gods?" he said. "You

can act as if you did have them!" And so he para-phrased the dictum of an old German philosopher who could never have dreamed that his words would live again under an enormous red sun at the end of time.

"Once your gods did not exist!" he said. "So the people created them! Your own religion says that! I asked Namalee why, if you did this once, you can't do it again, and she said that it was all right in the old days but is no longer permitted! Very well! But your gods are not *destroyed!* They are only *absent!* They have been stolen! So what is to prevent you from stealing them back?

"After all, a god is a god even if he does not dwell in the house of his worshippers! And who knows, it is highly probable that Zoomashmarta allowed this ca-lamity to fall in order to test you. If you find courage in yourselves, and go after Zoomashmarta and take him back, then you have passed the test! But if you sit around a fire and sorrow until your grief kills you, then you have failed!"

Namalee stood up and said, "What would you have us do?"

"You need a man to lead you who does not think quite as you do!" Ishmael said. "I will lead you! I will make new weapons, if I can find the materials, weap-ons such as no men have known for ages! Or if these weapons cannot be made, then we will depend on stealth and cunning! But I will ask a price for leading you."

"What is that price?" Namalee said.

"You will make me your Grand Admiral," Ishmael said.

He did not feel it necessary to add that he wanted to find a home. He had traveled enough and seen too much to desire more travel and more wonders.

"And you, Namalee, will be my wife," he said.

The captains and the officers did not know what to say. This was the first time that a stranger had asked to be elected as Grand Admiral. Didn't he know that Grand Admirals were born into the title? Or, if one died without a son, then the new one was chosen from the ranks of the greatest captains?

And how could he have the effrontery to ask that the daughter of a Grand Admiral be his mate?

Namalee, however, seemed to be happy, and Ishmael knew that he had guessed correctly. She *was* attracted to him. She might even be in love with him. It was difficult to say at this stage, since the women of Zalarapamtra were taught to be very self-controlled. But she had not told anyone of his attempts to kiss her or their keeping each other warm at nights. And while this restraint might have been caused by gratitude for his having saved her, he liked to think it was more than that.

There was silence for a long time. The men had looked at Namalee and had seen that she was not offended. Far from it. Then they had looked back at Ishmael and had seen a man strong and unafraid.

Finally, Daulhamra, the greatest of the captains now that Baramha was dead, rose. He stared around the room and then said, "Zalarapamtra dies unless it gets new blood. It needs this stranger who claims to be the grandson of long-dead ages. Perhaps he *has* been sent by the gods. If we accept him, then we use the gift of the gods. If we reject him, we deserve to die. I say behold the Grand Admiral!"

And thus Ishmael, who had never had any such ambitions, who had been content to be only a fo'cs'le hand, surpassed the dreams of his most ambitious bunkmates.

From that time on, it was as if he transmitted courage to them. They no longer walked around with downcast eyes and muttered when they talked or squatted for hours staring silently at the ruins. Now they moved briskly and talked much and loudly and laughed. This would not last long, Ishmael knew, unless he kept them moving with words and example. So he went down to the eternally quaking ground and the shaking jungle to search for *ghajashri*. This was the plant which burned so furiously and the smoke of which had an odor of stone-oil. Ishmael collected great quantities. In a large chamber of the city, he crushed the vegetation between two millstones the sailors had made under his direction. The pressure squeezed out a dark oily substance which caught fire quickly in the open. When the *ghajashri* oils were kept in a skin bag, their vapors accumulated. A burning fuse would set a bag of the oil off with a roar, and the oil would splash far and burn fiercely.

Ishmael set everybody who could be spared to collecting the plant and pressing out and collecting the oil. Since it took enormous quantities of the vegetation to get a small amount of oil, the work was long and hard. Meantime, two more whalers came home, and it was necessary to convince these newcomers that the pale-skinned, pale-eyed stranger was the new Grand Admiral.

Ishmael had expected that he and Namalee would be married very soon. But he quickly learned that the marriage would take place only after Zoomashmarta and the little gods had been rescued. A Grand Admiral never took his first bride until he had performed some heroic feat. Usually, this was the successful harpooning of ten whales or of twenty sharks in one day or leading a raid on an enemy city or an enemy ship and capturing it.

Ishmael, to prove his ability, would have to do what no man before him had ever done.

Ishmael then ordered a ship built which would be

twice the size of the largest so far. As usual, the Zala-rapamtrans did not jump to obey but wanted to know the reasons for his orders.

"It is true that there is no cause to build larger ships for hunting the whales," he said. "But this ship is a warship. With it I plan to destroy a whole city. Or at least a good part of it. It needs to be built as soon as possible because it will have to start out far ahead of the rest of the fleet. It will be so heavily loaded it will go very slowly."

The other ships had to have repairs and had to be stocked. And his men had to be trained for the raid into Booragangah. Also, the city had to be kept stocked with food.

Namalee's sisters and half-sisters insisted that they must accompany the ships on the expedition. Otherwise, they said, the ships would not have good luck.

Ishmael argued against this. If a ship went down, it took with it an invaluable and irreplaceable asset, a future mother. It was going to take long enough as it was to build the city into a strong and populous community nation again. If any more women were lost, the regrowth of Zalarapamtra might be impossible.

Reason said that Ishmael was right. Custom said he was wrong. Custom, as usual, won. Not only would one of Namalee's sisters be going for each ship going, but she would be on the flagship.

Ishmael did not argue any more. He could do just so much with these people. After that, he was wasting his breath and also losing his authority.

He worked as hard as anybody and harder than most. His hours for sleeping were not as many as he wished. It was difficult at first to sleep during the long day, when he knew that there was light to work by. The original cycle of eight hours of sleep and sixteen of waking still conducted men's lives. The lengthening of day and night had not interfered with that rhythm. These people were born to the practice of sleeping part of the daytime and working part of the nighttime. He found it a practice to which he, accustomed to strange hours of on-watch and off-watch, soon became adjusted.

The time came when the great ship was built and loaded with supplies and the cargo of fire-oil bombs. The ten men who were to crew it said goodbye and the mammoth vessel, the *Woobarangu*, lifted slowly, its sails spread, its goal the city of Booragangah thousands of miles to the northwest.

Four of the whaling vessels followed it five days later, that is, twenty of the days of Earth when its sun was white-hot. Ishmael commanded the *Roolanga*, the flagship. They were headed for a group of mountains which Ishmael thought had once been the Hawaiian Islands, though he could not be sure. In all the millions of years, possibly a billion or more, islands must have sunk and new ones risen and in turn been eroded to nothing and other islands taken their place. And all this long before the oceans dried up.

Sailing at an average of ten knots ground speed, the fleet could have reached its destination in about two hundred hours or two days and nights. But Ishmael had ordered that supplies be very short, since he wanted to use all the space he could for bombs and weapons. Thus, it was necessary on the second day to hunt whales to add to the food supply. And they were held up again when they caught up with the giant *Woobarangu*. They trimmed their sails to keep pace with it. When they were several hundred miles outside Booragangah, they began to circle, waiting until another long night began.

At the same time, they kept a sharp watch for enemy

sails, since whaling ships could be coming from any direction this close to the city.

The giant red disk finally dropped, its weak rays turning the distant top of the mountain that was their goal to a purplish point.

The captain of the other ships had boarded Ishmael's for the last conference. Once more, he made sure that each understood his part. Then they drank a toast in *shahamchiz* and departed. They looked pale but determined. The existence of their nation depended upon them, and their nation could not afford to lose even one of them, no matter if all the gods were restored. Moreover, if they were taken alive, they would suffer horrible torture. The enemy knew how to drag out agony and put off the end of it as the sun knew how to drag out the light.

As if stuck in the throat of night, the sun hung on the horizon. Then it was swallowed and in a moonless night the ships ceased circling and beat to the wind toward the distant spire. After an hour the top of the moon rose leprously above the east horizon and quickly flooded the dark with a bright illumination. It shone dully on the sails, which had been dyed black, and on the hull, also black. A second deck had been added to the bridge. This projected above the top of the hull and increased wind resistance, but it couldn't be helped. The captain and the steersmen had to see where they were going.

At an estimated hundred miles from Booragangah, all except the flagship began to circle upward. They would rise as high as they could, their crews breathing from wooden flasks of compressed air which Ishmael had designed. They would then sail to a point above their destination and begin circling again. After an hour, as regulated by the sand clocks Ishmael had made, they would descend. They would do this slowly until they

saw the signal, after which they would release gas swiftly. The great *Woobarangu* would discharge its gas
even more swiftly.

The *Roolanga* continued straight ahead, steadily descending. When it was about twenty feet above the
tops of the shivering vegetation, it leveled out. Long before the other ships had reached the top of their spiral,
it was sliding along quietly and slowly into the wind,
its sails furled, its lower mast drawn up. Grappling hooks
dragged through the jungle, making more noise than
Ishmael cared for. But eventually the hooks caught, and
men swarmed down the lines and secured them to
plants.

They were at the foot of the towering mountain, below the huge shelf on the top of which the city of the
enemy rested. Above them small sentinel boats circled,
and behind them ships nosed this way and that, looking for attackers or spies. But these had not been high
enough or low enough.

Ishmael had put on his dark clothes and blacked his
face. A moment later, Namalee, similarly dressed and
darkened, joined him. Ishmael gave his final instructions to Pavashtri, the first mate, who would be in com-
mand while Ishmael was gone. Then he and the girl
went down a ladder to the main walkway and along it
to a whaling boat port. There were six others who
would go with them in the boat, since this had been
built especially large. It strained against its moorings,
the bladders having been fed earlier until they had
made enough gas for a swift rising. The crew climbed
aboard and strapped themselves in. Each wore in a
sheath a long sharp knife made of a bamboo-like plant.
Their short spears and short stout bows and quivers
of arrows were in leather cases on the bottom of the
boat. The bows were something that Ishmael had had
to force on the Zalarapamtrans. They knew about them

but despised them for some reason lost in their past. Men did not use them, they said. Ishmael had replied that in his time—stretching time a little but for a good cause—bows were very manly indeed. The point was that they were deadly and the pathetically tiny party invading Booragangah needed all the firepower it could get. Ishmael knew this was true because the gods had said so.

By this time, Ishmael was not above telling them that he knew what their gods wanted of them. He acted as if he were receiving divine commands by thought transmission, and the others began to act as if he were. Perhaps they did so because they wanted to believe that their gods had not entirely deserted them.

There were no lights permitted aboard, of course, so the signal to release all six boats simultaneously was passed by yanking on a system of lines rigged for the occasion through the ship.

The lines restraining the boats were slashed, and sailors shoved the boats out before they would rise and get stuck in the hull. The side of a boat bumped against the upper part of the wide port as it shot up. A sailor was feeding the amorphous mostly-mouth beasts at the necks of the bladder, and these were manufacturing the gas to increase the buoyancy even as the boat ascended.

The moon had passed below the western horizon before the *Roolanga* had entered the final fifty miles of her journey. The immense shelf above placed the small boats in shadow. The front of the mountain, a vertical cliff here, went by at a distance of several hundred yards. The boats, their sails folded and the masts and arms shipped and folded, rose at the mercy of the wind. This was slight at this point, so the boats drifted about half a mile before they were just below the overhang. Karkri, in charge of maneuvering, began to let the gas out. The other boats also slowed their ascent.

The men in charge were born to the air. Almost without thinking, they estimated to an inch the amount of buoyancy to lose. The top of the fat oval ring that formed the outer part of the boat bumped against the stone. The people in it were stretched out flat on their faces, but even so outcrops scraped against the backs of some. Then the crews turned over on their backs and propelled the boat slowly outward by reaching up and grabbing the rough stone and pushing.

It was slow and laborious work, since the shelf projected for a half mile from where they had first struck it. And they could not go swiftly if they had wished to. It was a matter of pulling and hoping the scraping of the hull against the rough stone would not abrade through the skin. The skin was tough but very thin for the sake of lightness.

Above the hard breathings of the crew Ishmael heard a hissing from the boat behind and to the right of them. Ishmael told the others to stop, and the boat slid to a halt, pressing against the rock bottom. To see what was going on, it was necessary to push against the rock to lower the boat. Ishmael squirmed around while everybody else pushed. The boat to the right was about six feet away and was only a dim shape in the blackness.

Vargajampa, the third mate, said softly, "*Joognaja!* There is a shaft in the rocks here!"

"What size?" Ishmael called back. He hoped that there was no one listening at the upper end of the shaft.

"Just large enough! There is a grille of wood in the opening, however!"

Ishmael gave the order, and his crew began working the boat toward the other, while that one moved away.

He had had two plans for entering the city. One was to come up from under and slip over the edge and then enter from above. The second plan was to come up from beneath through one of the ventilation shafts, if one could be found in the dark and if it was large enough to admit a man.

Namalee had told him that, as far as she knew, no one had ever penetrated into an enemy's city in this manner. In fact, though raids had been made at night, they were always either sudden massive onslaughts or a few ships sailing in, destroying, looting and then getting away as swiftly as possible. No one had ever carried out such a plan as Ishmael's or even suggested it.

Despite this, however, the possibility of such was recognized. That explained why the shafts were screened and sometimes guarded.

When the boat was centered under the shaft, Ishmael gripped the latticework of wood set into it and pulled. The grille failed to yield. By probing through the spaces between the bars with a slender stick, he determined that a rope was secured with hard wooden pegs to each corner on the inside of the screen. The other end of the ropes must be secured to the inside of a grille set in the top end of the shaft. It was possible that a pull on this grille would drag the other down and set off an alarm mechanism.

To avoid this, he inserted a slender stick with a flint knife on one end and cut the ropes. Then, after some hard pulling and prying with a sharp stick, he managed to get the grille loose. He stood up slowly and pulled himself up by one of the ropes into the shaft. After that, to avoid pulling the grille loose, and so precipitating himself down the shaft, he braced himself against the walls. It was not easy to climb in that manner. The tunnel was so narrow that he had to hold himself in, and progress upward, by using his knees, and shove upward a few inches. This would have taken the skin off his back and knees and hands if he had not clothed himself in thin leather and put on thin leather gloves. Nevertheless, before he got to the top, the leather was worn through. And he was puffing and panting and sweating and trembling. On reaching the top, he waited until his breathing had become inaudible. He listened for sounds: a foot scraping against the stone, snoring, heavy breathing, but could hear nothing except the blood in his ears.

The grille above him came out with a skreaking that tore at his nerves as the stone had torn at his leather clothes. He waited a while after it had come loose and then inched up, expecting to have his head split open by a stone ax when it emerged. But there was no one waiting for him. He lit a match and looked around. The room, a cube cut out of rock, was empty except for some boxes in one corner.

He hoisted himself out and lay for a moment on the floor, which trembled beneath him. When he rose, he went to the open doorway and looked down it but could see nothing because of the darkness. He returned to the shaft and uncoiled the rope bound about his waist. It fell down the shaft and was seized by someone below and given a tug. Ishmael sat down, holding the rope, his feet braced against the opposite lip of the shaft. He held on while Namalee climbed up it. After she was out, she helped him hold the rope while Karkri came up.

Karkri and she held the rope while the next sailor came up.

Ishmael took a small torch Namalee had carried up in a sack. He lit it and then proceeded down the hall corridor. The open entrances on either side gave to more storerooms. At one end, the corridor stopped against stone; at the other, it opened into a stairway cut out of the rock. This curved around and up. Ishmael decided not to go any further until all of the men had come up the shaft. This was a slow process. The empty boats had to be slid away, and the balancing of each boat required a careful moving around. Every time a man went up a shaft, the equilibrium of the boat was affected.

One boat was to remain with three men aboard. These would wait until three hours had passed. If the others had not returned by then, the three were to take their boat back to the *Roolanga* and the next phase would begin.

Ishmael led the band to the next level, which was much like the lower one. The corridor, however, was twice as long as the one beneath it. And the one above that was double the length of the one below it.

Booragangah seemed to be built much as Zalarapamtra was. This, too, would have had an upside-down pyramid-like appearance if a cross-section had been cut in it. The next level should be twice as long as the one below it, and it was. This, however, was lit here and there with torches or with the less bright but low-oxygen-using fireflies. The torches or cages were set in stone rings carved out of the wall. The few people within were sleeping.

These, Namalee whispered, would be slaves. Normally there would be no one even on this level during sleep-time, but they must be here because they had work to do. The rooms unoccupied by people were filled with neatly stacked boxes. There were also piles along the corridors, waiting to be carried into the rooms.

They passed on. It might have been best to kill the slaves, but there was always the chance that one would wake and cry out. And these were not going to attack the invaders if they should be forced back this way.

They would stand to one side and let invaders and invaded fight it out.

The Zalarapamtrans proceeded more swiftly. The fact that the layout of the tunnels was much like that of their own city assured them that they could find the way to the temple. They went up the next stairway and turned to the left to go in toward the mountain. But Ishmael and two others went ahead without torches and with knives ready while the others waited below. This corridor was dark, and a few random explorations of chambers along the way disclosed more storerooms, one of them an arsenal. These contained no weapons which the band did not have.

The party went to the other end of the corridor. This did not end in a wall, as the others did, but in another staircase. Namalee said that she expected this, since the corridor of her city on this level also had a staircase.

"This should lead up to another corridor at the end of which is another stairway to still another corridor. But that one will lead to the temple of the gods. Only . . ."

"Only what?" Ishmael said.

"A long time ago, when even my great-grandparents were not yet born, a Zalarapamtran escaped from Booragangah. He told some strange stories. One says that there are guardians of the temple of the gods of Booragangah. Not human guardians. Beasts that the founder of this city, the hero Booragangah himself, could not kill. So he left them here in places where the unwary would encounter them, and—"

"We've no time for folk tales," Ishmael said. But when he had climbed the next staircase and looked around the corner, he was not so sure that there was not something strange in this place.

This hallway, unlike the others, was brightly lit.

Torches and cages of fireflies were set within stone rings every six feet, two cages for every torch. The hallway ran deep into the shelf, or into the mountain, for he was not certain how deeply they had penetrated. At the far end the corridor tilted upward. The lower end was still visible, however, and something across it flickered brightly in the torchlight.

Ishmael finally stepped out from around the corner. The air passed across his face like a cold hand. At the junction of wall and floor were many holes about six inches across. Apparently these were shafts drilled through to the bottom of the shelf. He did not know what caused the air to move. What did come to him was a vision of the ledge drilled through with many holes and the tiny cracks that had to be developed in the ledge with the constant vibration of earthtides and quakes and the cracks spreading and reaching the shafts and then, inevitably, a great piece of the ledge falling off.

He walked ahead of the others, while those who had been given bows strung them. It was time for them, now that they were approaching a place where they knew the enemy would be up and armed.

The end of the corridor behind them was a blank wall, and there were no doorways or archways along the walls. They passed by the torches and caged fireflies and started up the slope. At the end was a square-cornered opening about seven feet high and six feet wide. Across it was a spiderwebbish arrangement of gray strands bearing little bits of mica-like material. It was these that flickered in the shifting light of the torches.

"What is that?" Ishmael whispered.

"I do not know," Namalee said.

Ishmael took a torch from a man and stepped up close to the web and peered through it. The torch threw the shadow of the strands onto the floor behind it. Beyond was a vast darkness.

Ishmael hesitated. The web looked so fragile that he could not imagine why it had been set there. Or would breaking it set off an alarm, as the shaking of a spider's web transmitted vibrations to the waiting predator? If he burned it with his torch, and so avoided touching it, he still might release tension on strands connected to the web and leading back into the darkness. And the release of tension would awaken something in there.

He could not stand there much longer. To show indecisiveness or hesitancy was to lessen the others' belief in him, and this was all that had brought them here and the only thing that would keep them here.

He passed the torch across the face of the web and the flames licked them out of existence. The mica-stuff fell to the floor like metallic snowflakes.

A thrumming sound, faint but deep, came from the darkness.

Holding the torch ahead of him, Ishmael stepped through the doorway.

The light opened its own path. The room was even larger than he had thought. The ceiling was so high that the torchlight could not reach to it, and the walls receded at a slant into invisibility. Before him was a smooth stone floor that stretched into the heart of the mountain, or at least looked as if it did.

The air, however, was motionless, musty and warm. There were no shafts sunk along the walls.

The others came through the entrance and gathered behind him. Four held torches, and these pushed the darkness back more. But the ceiling was still shrouded, and the walls departed to the right and the left at an ever-increasing angle.

Namalee spoke very softly behind him. "It is said that

when Booragangah led his people to this place, he found that others had lived here before him. There were some large chambers cut into the mountain itself and some perilous beasts living in them. The original inhabitants had died out or been killed by the perilous beasts. Booragangah slew some, but the others were too strong for him. So he shut them up, and his people cut other rooms and halls into the rock of the great ledge."

"Doubtless the story contains some elements of truth," Ishmael said. "But if there are any beasts here, they do not seem to have been shut up. How could that web hold anything in?"

"I do not know," she said. "But it might have an odor that we can't detect but that the beast can. Or there may be some other explanation."

Their whispers seemed to fly out like bats into a never-ending night. The darkness was absorbent; it sucked in everything, light, sound and, given a chance, it might suck in their bodies.

Ishmael, stepping forward again, holding the torch above him, was reminded that he really knew little of this world. Though he had crossed vast distances on it and seen strange things, he had become accustomed to much of it. But there must be many sinister things in this world, things which he would be ill-prepared to cope with because he would not understand their nature.

He went on. The torches were burning ships falling in the night. Darkness split ahead of them and fused behind them. And the stillness and silence continued.

After a while, Ishmael got the impression that the darkness was breathing. It was as if the darkness were itself an entity, a gigantic animal without form which lived on all sides of them.

Ishmael looked back at the doorway. It was a block

of light—but not the solid block it had been after he had burned off the web.

The web was back.

Namalee, who had also looked back, gasped.

The others turned their heads too.

"It may be some small animal which spins a web as soon as it is broken," Ishmael said. He tried to say it as if he meant it.

He turned away and began walking forward again. It would have been easy to panic then and dash toward the doorway and the web. Perhaps, though, that was what the spinner hoped they would do. In any event, they must go on.

Something whooshed by his head.

He spun, batting at it with his torch.

A round body, grayish in the light, with six thin legs and a round head with a big eye and a slit mouth from which a long sharp tooth stuck, sailed away into the darkness. Its body was about the size of his own head, and something very thin and slimy was emerging from its back. Then he realized that the thin slimy thing was a line, and that the other end was attached to the ceiling somewhere up there in the black. The creature had leaped out, probably from high up on a wall, and swung down and made a pass at his head.

He said, "Get down! Look above!" and got down on one knee. "Don't scream, whatever happens!"

These beasts might be quite harmless except as watch dogs to frighten away intruders or to cause them to make a noise which would alert the human sentinels.

The next creature came out of the darkness on the end of its line so swiftly that there was no defense. It shot out into the light and fastened its legs around the head of a sailor near Ishmael. The impact knocked the man backward, and his short spear clattered on the stone. The man next to him stabbed his spear into the creature, which spread out its six legs and fell off its victim's head. It lay on the floor, kicking.

The sailor did not get up.

Ishmael shook him and placed his head against his heart and then peeled back an eyelid.

"He's dead."

There were three little red marks on the man's neck where the claws at the end of the legs had scratched.

Something dark gray shot out of the darkness, and another sailor impaled it on his spear.

The spear was torn out of the man's grasp, but the thing was dead.

About thirty seconds later, another arced over their heads, but it went on into the darkness.

That the creatures didn't swing back showed that they were ending their swing on something hanging down from the ceiling.

Ishmael counted to twenty slowly and then told everybody to roll a few feet to one side immediately. At approximately thirty seconds after the last thing had swung over, another zoomed over them. It was lower to the floor than the previous one but not low enough because of the change of position of its intended prey.

There might be thousands of them—a chilling vision—but they seemed to be taking turns at thirty-second intervals.

Ishmael leaped up and threw the torch high into the air.

It turned over and over, lighting up only darkness, until it came to the top of its arc. It briefly illuminated the ends of three thick strands of grayish stuff hanging down from the darkness. The ceiling was still out of sight. But on each strand, clinging to it, was one of the creatures.

Ishmael could not see it, but he suspected that a grayish line coming from the back of each creature was attached at the other end to the hanging strand. It seemed likely that the line was coiled inside the thing's body and could be controlled for the distance needed for the deadly swing at its prey on the floor.

The creatures did not drop; they seemed paralyzed by the torchlight.

But there must be many others outside the light who were not frozen by it.

For some reason, through some complex of interactions, uncoiling from their instincts, which were habits formed and fossilized millions of years ago, they dropped at thirty-second intervals. Something passed through them, releasing them at stated intervals like so many wooden cuckoos.

Ishmael told the crew in a low voice that they were to run. But they should imitate him, and when he leaped to one side, they must do so too. And when he dropped to the floor, they must do the same.

He set out immediately, starting his count at fifteen, which was his rough estimate of the time it had taken him to give his orders. At thirty he threw himself on the floor, reaching out at the same time to seize the fallen torch, which had landed about thirty feet from where he had cast it.

The gray six-legged thing arced over him and into the darkness.

Ishmael got up, counting under his breath, and ran forward. At the count of thirty, he gave two tremendous leaps to the left, and the torches showed a dark body hurtling through the light and on up.

The next time he slashed upward, and his spearhead, though it missed the creature, severed the line from its back. It was just starting the upward swing and so flew out of sight. But a moment later, having dashed ahead, Ishmael saw it. It was staggering around, two of its thin legs bent outward. Even so, it scuttled away and would have been lost-if a sailor had not thrown a torch after it. The brand hit the floor, bounced, cartwheeling, and its flaming end struck the thing. An odor of burned flesh was wafted to them; the thing folded its unbroken legs to its body and died, or pretended to die. Ishmael made certain with his spear.

All that time, he did not cease counting. And so it was by the numbers that he led his band to safety, to the entrance to another room which was also covered by a glittering web. He burned this and ran through. The last thing to swing down made a desperate effort which brought it with a splopping against the wall just above the lintel. It fell down shattered, oozing a pale green liquid in the light of the torch thrust over it by the last man. Ishmael spoke softly but urgently, telling him not to waste time.

The next room did not reveal to the thrown torch anything like they had just left. It seemed to be nothing except a black emptiness. That did not mean the room was bare: the light had not reached the ceiling or the walls.

Ishmael looked back toward the doorway through which they had escaped, hoping to see the doorway on the other side of the room, the first they had entered, still limned with faint light. It would be a sort of lighthouse, assuring him that they were not in a universe which had gone eternally dark.

He did see the rectangle, or its ghost, far off.

He also saw something else. Rather, he saw the lack of something.

"Where is Pamkamshi?" he said.

The others looked back too. Then they looked at each other.

"He was behind me a moment ago," Goonrajum, a sailor. said.

"I thought he was carrying a torch," Ishmael said. "But you have one now. Did he give you his?"

"He asked me to hold it for a moment," Goonrajum said.

And now Pamkamshi was gone.

Ishmael and the others, keeping close together, retraced their path until they were close to the doorway. This was again covered by a web.

Ishmael led them away from the door but on a winding path calculated to cover territory at random. Nowhere was there any sign of Pamkamshi.

Again Ishmael threw his torch high into the air.

He saw nothing, except . . . But he could not be sure.

He picked up the torch and threw it once more, putting every bit of force he had into the throw.

The torch, just before beginning its downward arc, illuminated palely something that might or might not be two bare feet.

"Listen!" Namalee said.

They were quiet. The torches sputtered and flickered. Ishmael could hear his own blood singing. And he could hear another sound, very faintly.

"It sounds like somebody chewing," Namalee said.

"Chomping," Karkri said.

At Ishmael's request, Karkri took the torch and cast it upward. Though he was shorter and lighter in weight than Ishmael, he still had spent half of his life throwing a harpoon. The torch sailed up higher than when Ishmael had thrown it, and it showed a pair of bare feet hanging in the air. They were moving slowly away from the men below.

Namalee gasped, and some of the men uttered prayers or curses.

"Something snatched Pamkamshi into the air when nobody had their eyes on him," Ishmael said. "Something up there."

He felt cold, and his stomach muscles were contracting.

"Shoot up in that direction," he said to Avarjam, who had a bow. "Don't worry about hitting Pamkamshi. I think he is dead. His feet weren't moving by themselves. Something is carrying him off across the room."

Avarjam shot an arrow into the darkness above them. The string thrummed, and then there was a thudding noise. The arrow did not clatter on the floor ahead of them.

"You hit something," Ishmael said, wondering if it was Pamkamshi. Perhaps the arrow had driven into a man who was only unconscious, not dead. But he could not help that. The safety of the greater number and of the mission was paramount.

They walked on ahead until Ishmael ordered a stop. Karkri again threw the torch up, and this time it showed not only the feet but the legs. The upper part of Pamkamshi, however, was as shrouded as if he had been buried.

"He's lower than he was," Ishmael said, and then there was a loud thump ahead of them. They hurried forward and saw in the torchlight the body of Pamkamshi. His bones were broken and his flesh burst open. But it was not the fall that had killed him. Around his neck was a broad purplish mark, and his eyes bulged out and his tongue protruded. Something had eaten his scalp and ears and part of his nose.

"Everybody put one hand up by their necks and keep them there until I say to do otherwise," Ishmael said.

"What did the arrow hit?" Namalee said.

She looked up and yelled, forgetting Ishmael's orders to keep quiet, and jumped back. They looked too, and they jumped away, opening out.

The creature that fell onto the stone floor by Pam-

113

kamshi was pancake-shaped and bore a great suction pad on its back and on the other side a coil of purplish hue by a great mouth with many small teeth. The arrow had run half its length through it and probably pinned it to the ceiling after its death had released the huge suction pad.

The beast had dropped its long tentacle nooselike around the neck of Pamkamshi and snatched him into the upper darkness. Whether it had selected the man because he was being unobserved by the others or whether it was by accident, Ishmael did not know. But he suspected that the beast possessed some organs of perceptions not apparent to those unfamiliar with the creature.

He also suspected that the ceiling was crowded with the beasts and that he and his band were in deadly peril. If this was true, however, something was preventing the beasts from making a mass attack. Did there exist among them, as he suspected there did among the creatures of the room they had just quitted, a communal mind? Or, if not a mind, some sort of common nervous system? And this allotted to each in its turn a chance to try for a victim? Or did the hypothesized common agreement insist that any beast could attack when it was safe for one to do so? And what was the safety rule? That one of the prey should be unobserved momentarily by his fellows?

If this was the rule, then the creatures were vulnerable in some respect; otherwise they would not care whether or not the intended victim was isolated from his group.

Ishmael leaned over the thing to study the effects of the arrow. A pale green fluid had spread out from the wound, which was centered on a lump in the body about the size and shape of an ostrich egg. Ishmael thought that this could be one of its vital organs.

There were about fifty of the eggish lumps in the body. The rest was apparently occupied by little but fatty tissue and a circulatory system, though this was only his guess.

Ishmael straightened up and signaled that they should proceed. They all kept one hand by their necks, and they kept glancing upward, as if they expected to see a purplish tentacle drop into the illuminated world of the torches.

After walking sixty paces, Ishmael stopped them again and again Karkri tossed a torch upward. The light flared briefly on a dozen tentacles uncoiling slowly from the darkness above.

Ishmael had no idea of what was causing this concerted action now. Perhaps the beasts, in whatever form of communication they used, had conferred and decided that individual action was a failure. Or perhaps the death of one resulted in triggering an instinct which activated them to a communal effort.

Ishmael gave an order, and the band ran forward. They stayed together, however, and each kept a hand by his neck. They had not gone forty steps before a dozen tentacles shot like frogs' tongues down from the blackness. Each dropped around a neck and its neighboring hand and tightened.

Namalee was one of those caught.

Ishmael spun around at the cries of those seized. He barked an order to the archers to crouch close to the floor, and to fire upward at random as best they could in this position. They were safer from attack now than if they had been standing up. And they sent shaft after shaft into the upper darkness.

Ishmael picked up a torch that had been dropped by a man who was now struggling to keep from being lifted by the tentacle. His hand kept the tentacle from strangling him immediately, but his face was turning bluish-black in the light.

Ishmael rammed the torch against the tentacle, and it released the man and snapped upward and out of sight. The odor of burned flesh trailed from it as smoke from a rocket.

Ishmael leaped upward, grabbing the slimy, ropy limb that was hauling Namalee upward. His weight pulled them both down, and with his other hand he passed the surface of the torch along the tentacle. It uncoiled and dropped them both on the stone floor.

By then the othe torch-bearers were burning the tentacles, and these uncoiled and withdrew.

Something heavy struck the floor ahead of them. After reorganizing, they proceeded ahead and shortly their lights flickered on a dead beast. An arrow had pierced one of the lumpy organs.

Torch men stood on the periphery of the group and waved the brands wildly. A single torchman in the center of the group waved his brand. Ishmael hoped by this positioning of the torches to discourage the beasts. Within forty yards they saw the wall of the chamber and a small square opening. They ran into it, though Ishmael would have liked to have gone slowly and cautiously. The builders of this place may have anticipated that those who ran the gantlet of the tentacles would dive headlong into this entrance as a mouse goes into a hole when the cat is after it.

But there was, by then, no appealing to the better sense of the group.

Their torches showed them a corridor that curved to the right. It was wide enough for two to go abreast and the ceiling was two men high. It continued to curve to the right for about eighty paces and then curved to the left. After about a hundred paces, they came to a stairway cut out of stone. This was so narrow that they would have to go in single file. The ascent was very steep, and the walls curved to the right.

Ishmael led the way, holding a torch in one hand and a spear in the other. As he ascended, he wondered how far these chambers of horrors extended. It was possible that they went on and on and finally ended in a blank wall or in some trap which no one could possibly escape. But he did not see how the Booragan-gahns could afford to stock these rooms with very many guardians. The beasts could not subsist on trespassers alone. It was doubtful that anybody had penetrated into this area since the chambers had been carved. To keep the guardians alive, the Booragangahns had to feed them. And even if the beasts existed most of the time in a dormant state, they still had to be fed from time to time. From the viewpoint of economy alone, the beasts had to be limited in number.

Presently the narrow stairway straightened out. Ishmael kept on climbing and, when he had counted three hundred, he stopped.

Above was the top of the stairs. And on it squatted a huge stone figure.

It was gray and shaped something like a tortoise with a frog's head and a badger's legs. The highest point, the crest of the tortoise shell, was about four feet from the floor. It quivered with the eternal shaking of the rock, and this motion gave it a semblance of life.

The eyes were as gray and stonelike as the rest of the body.

But when Ishmael got close enough to look into one of the eyes, he thought he saw it swivel within the eye socket.

His nerves were slipping their moorings, he thought, and he stepped into the hall which the figure guarded.

The stone head turned with a creaking.

Had it not been for the noise, Ishmael would have

been caught unawares and the stone jaws would have closed on his arm.

He jumped away and the jaws clanged shut as if they were made of iron.

At the same time, the body lifted on its badgerish legs and started to turn.

Ishmael rammed his spear into the mouth, when the jaws opened again.

A yellowish fluid sprayed out of the mouth into Namalee's face and she fell backward against the man on the step below her. Ishmael leaped up and jumped up onto the thing's back. He pulled out his stone knife and began chipping away at its right eye. His knife shattered, and then the neck of the thing creaked as it slid far out from the shell. Ishmael could no longer reach the head to stab at it, and it dipped to get at Namalee.

The people behind Namalee had retreated but one man, Karkri, sent an arrow into the thing's open mouth.

The head continued to approach Namalee, the neck seeming to be of interminable length. Ishmael could see that the neck was of stone, or covered with stone. But the silicon consisted of hundreds of tiny plates, and these slid one over the other as the thing moved its neck from side to side and bent it downward.

Ishmael stood up on the tortoise-shaped shell and leaped outward. He came down astraddle the extended neck just behind the massive head. His weight carried the neck and head down until the head slammed into the steps. More yellowish fluid spurted out from the thing's open mouth, and then abruptly the jet became a trickle.

There was no more movement from the creature.

Ishmael got off the neck and slid down alongside the head. The gray hard eyes were as stony and lifeless as before, but this time the thing seemed to be actually dead. The mouth was still open, and a torch showed that Ishmael's spear and Karkri's arrow had pierced a huge eyeball-like organ in the cavity past the throat. This no longer pulsed, though some of the yellowish fluid was still oozing out from around the shafts of the two weapons. Ishmael asked Namalee if she had been hurt, and she replied that only her emotions were pained. Then he rapped on the thing's hide. If the skin of the beast was not indeed granite, it was something very like it. What manner of beast was this that excreted a skin which hardened into stone?

Namalee and the others said that they had never heard of such a creature, not even in the many tales of horrible beasts they had heard from their grandmothers.

"But it is dead now," Ishmael said. "I do not know where the Booragangahns got this creature. I suppose they may have found it buried in the heart of the mountain when they carved these steps. I hope this was the only one they found. At least we will not have to worry about it on the way back."

"Do not be so sure," Karkri said.

He held his torch in the thing's mouth, and Ishmael saw that the arrow and the spear were being sucked—or absorbed—into the red organ. And the thing was beginning to pulse again. Or was that an illusion fostered by the eternal shaking of this world?

Then the jaws slowly closed, and the neck began to retract. The gray eyes continued to stare as blankly, and the head offered no hostility. But the men scrambled by it, watching it closely to make sure that the head did not turn toward them. When they were all in the hallway, behind the back of the thing, they paused for a moment. They looked at Ishmael as if to ask, What next?

He said, "All we can do is go ahead. But I am sure of one thing: the priests of the temple of Boorangah will not be expecting anybody to come alive through here. So we will take them unawares."

"If this *does* lead to the temple," Vashgunammi, a sailor, said.

"Somebody has to feed the guardian beasts once in a while, and I doubt that they enter from the other end to do so," Ishmael said. "In any event, we must go on until we win or lose."

And that, he said to himself as he turned away, *summed up the mechanics of life.* A living being had to keep on going, no matter what happened, until the enemy was conquered or had conquered. Even here, in this quivering world of the red sun and the falling moon, that held true.

So far they had been fortunate. If the guardians had been more vigorous, or of a slightly more belligerent nature, they might have wiped out the band of invaders. And perhaps in earlier days they might have done so. But ages had passed with no call for their talents, and they had grown older and more feeble. Their keepers, the priests, had started to neglect them, perhaps not feeding them enough to keep them fully strong. And the beasts dwelt in the long, long darkness and dreamed of their prey; when their prey was among them, they took a long time awakening. The sluggishness of millennia was not easily overcome.

However, now that they were alert, they might be three times as dangerous if the invaders attempted to return this way.

Might be . . .

They were faced with another extremely steep stairway cut into the stone. This led up and up and then became even steeper with very high rises so that Ishmael's shins brushed against the edges of the steps. Presently he was clinging to the steps with his free hand while he held a torch in the other.

Since he had entered the chambers, Ishmael had looked for signs of the keepers: dust or lack of it, footprints or lack of them where they should be, anything that would show that these rooms were used. But there was no dust and therefore no footprints. And there was not a sign of garbage or of anything left after the animals had been fed. Apparently the priests ventured into here often enough to clean up. Or the priests only cleaned up at long intervals and they had just recently done so. Whatever the situation, the chambers must have been cleaned a short time ago.

Ishmael was heartened by this, because the chances were that the keepers would not be coming for some time. Also, the fact that the beasts had been fed recently might account for their lack of all-out fury. The edge of their hunger had been taken off.

Ishmael whispered, "Perhaps you are bringing us good luck, Namalee!"

"What did you say?" she whispered back.

"Nothing," he said, lifting his free hand to signal silence. He thought he had heard a noise from above.

The others stopped climbing too, and they stood on the steps, listening.

Again the faint noise drifted down the flight of stairs. It sounded something like chanting.

"I think we might be close to the temple," Namalee said.

"I hope we are close to the exit from this place," Karkri said. "Something is following us."

Ishmael looked back down the steps, past the torches, and strained to see into the darkness at the foot of the steps. The extreme influence of the torchlights barely reached there. Still, it was light enough for him to see the hulk that moved slowly, creakingly, from the corridor into the space at the bottom. Though he could not make out the details, he knew that it was the stone beast.

"It didn't die," Namalee said.

"And it's waiting for us," Ishmael said. "Well, it surely can't come up the steps after us."

The thing made no effort to ascend the flight. It was as motionless as the statue it seemed to be. It was waiting, and it probably was better at waiting than any creature in this world or the one that Ishmael had left.

"It's blocking the corridor," Karkri said. "And the next time it will be aroused. We have hurt it, and it won't forget that."

"You don't know that," Ishmael said.

He climbed on until he reached another narrow corridor. This led straight for about sixty feet and ended in a wall of stone. But the voices, which had become louder, had to be close by. He put his ear to the wall and could hear the chanting quite clearly. It was not in the tongue of the Zalarapamtrans.

Softly, he rapped on the wall. He was surprised to find that the wall was not as thin as he had thought. It was very thick and solid. He determined after going over the wall that the voices were filtering through openings near the bottom, the center, and the top of the wall. These were holes a quarter-inch wide drilled through the stone and spaced about a foot apart.

"They must move this wall somehow," Ishmael said to Namalee.

He pushed at various places and passed the torch over every inch of the wall and the adjacent areas of the corridor. But he could find nothing that might serve as a button or an activator to swing the wall on a pivot. He was convinced that this had to be the manner in which the wall was operated.

"Perhaps," Namalee said, "the mechanisms are all on the other side?"

"I hope not," he said, "though that would be one way of making sure that intruders did not get into the temple even if they escaped the guardians. To return after feeding the beasts, though, the priests would have to notify those on the other side of the wall to operate the mechanism. I suppose they could do so through the little holes."

"The stone beast is coming up after us," Karkri said.

Ishmael returned to the head of the stairs and looked down in the light of the torch Karkri held. It was true. The great shell of the beast was tilted upward, and the massive legs with the claws of stone were gripping the edges of a step. Slowly, and with a grinding noise, the bottom of the shell scraping against the steps, the monster pulled itself up. Its head was extended out of the shell and its jaws were opened wide. Ishmael went carefully down the steep steps until he was close enough to see into the wide yawn of the mouth. The eyeball thing inside pulsed much more rapidly than the first time he had seen it. And the arrow and spear seemed to have been absorbed into the organ. Possibly their wood had provided it with fuel. The beast's life must be comparable to a low and slow-burning fire under a tea kettle. The energy was low, but even a small fire will eventually make a kettle boil.

Ishmael went down several more steps until he was just out of reach of the beast if it should extend its neck to its limit. The head turned slightly to each side as if the thing wanted to give each of the gray granite eyes a view of its victim. Ishmael retreated one step and to do so had to turn his back on the thing. He grabbed the edge of the high riser and pulled; Namalee shrieked. Without looking back he pulled himself up swiftly and then turned.

The thing had come up more swiftly than he would have thought possible. A paw reached up and the dead-looking gray-rock claws hooked into the edge of the step. The second paw hooked, and the legs bent to pull the great body up. The hind legs spread out to brace itself. The neck slid back into the shell, but the mouth remained wide open.

Ishmael kept on retreating while the stone thing clambered after him. When he was near the top, Ishmael stopped. Once that monster came over the edge and had a stable footing on the corridor, it could advance on the party. And, due to the narrowness of the corridor, not more than two men could fight it at one time.

Ishmael turned and said, "Hurry up! Try to find how to get out, or . . ."

He didn't need to finish. The others could see what might happen. Karkri came to his side and looked down. He said, "The beast has a precarious hold."

"There's only one way to keep it from getting up here," Ishmael said.

They went down four steps and stood just out of reach of the head if the neck should extend further. They whispered together and then, as they saw the beast reach out its right paw to grip the next step, they leaped outward with all their force.

With a speed that neither man had reckoned on because they considered the creature to be of stone, and stone had to be slow, the neck thrust the head at them. It was fortunate only that the beast chose Karkri and not Ishmael. If it had been the other way, that head, launched on a neck as swift as a line singing out at the end of a harpoon deep in a whale just struck, would have closed its jaws on Ishmael.

But they ground down like millstones on Karkri's feet as he leaped forward.

Ishmael's feet struck the shell just beside the right side of the neck.

Karkri screamed as his leg bones were ground together and his back struck the edge of a step.

The monster, borne by the impact of the two bodies, rose up and backward. Its hind feet slipped and, still holding the screaming Karkri in its jaws, it fell back. Karkri was flipped up and over through the air as if he were a weight on the end of a cracked whip. He described an arc and smashed into the steps below the monster, which then fell upon him on its back.

Ishmael leaped down again and drove his feet against the side of the beast, which had turned as if on a pivot on the high part of the shell. His driving legs spun it on around and it slipped on the edge of another step and crashed down the steps. At the bottom it turned over and fell upon its back, and there it stayed, kicking its short legs, unable to get back onto its feet, just like a tortoise of flesh.

This time Karkri was almost on top of the beast. He lay face-down while blood ran from him down the steps and formed a pool around the shell of the beast's back.

Ishmael took a few seconds to determine that Karkri was past saving. He climbed back up the steps and returned to the wall. Though the beast had made a great crashing noise when it went down the steps, the noise had apparently not been heard on the other side of the wall. The chanting was louder than before.

"I almost wish that they had heard and came to investigate," Ishmael muttered. "At least we'd be able to get to the other side."

Everything that they could think to do had been done, and still they had discovered no means for opening the wall. They could not just sit there and wait because they would starve to death. Moreover, step two of the plan would be set into motion, and if Ishmael's band was within the temple the raid would be a failure. It still was not too late to return to the boats and try to enter from the upper part of the ledge. But Ishmael had no heart for that and neither, he was certain, did any of his band. Surely there was a key to entrance into the temple. It was just that they were ignorant or blind.

He looked through one of the shafts in the wall. There was a dim light on the other side the source of which he could not see. About twenty or so feet beyond the wall was another gray stone wall. The voices seemed to be coming from the right. He doubted that the chanters were in the room he was looking into, but the voices had to be close to penetrate the shafts.

Ishmael clamped his teeth together as if he were biting down on time to shake it, as a terrier shakes a rat.

"Perhaps we should put out the torches," Namalee said. "If they should go by the wall and see the light through the shafts . . ."

Ishmael cursed to himself because he had not thought of that. He ordered the torches doused with a heavy powder which one man carried in a pouch for this purpose. Another man carried a small bag of oil with which to soak the torches and matches of weed and chemicals derived from some ground plants. Ishmael checked that they still had these before he allowed the flames to be put out.

Then they were in darkness and silence. The voices had stopped.

Ishmael put his ear to a shaft. After a while he heard a cough. Despite his situation, he smiled. There was something comfortable and comforting in that cough. Doubtless the congregation, or choir, was silent while waiting for a final benediction or statement of dismissal. And, as always happened in a church meeting, some-one coughed.

The earth never stopped shaking and the seas were dried up, the sun was a giant dying and the moon was falling, and most of life had taken to the air, which was itself disappearing. But human nature had not changed as swiftly as the world in which it existed.

Then he lost the smile as someone shouted a few words and there was the sound of many feet shuffling and a murmur of voices. The meeting was breaking up.

A minute later a torch brightened the room on the other side of the wall, feet shuffled, and two men talk-ing in low voices, one holding a torch, went by. They were robed and hooded in a scarlet material and would have passed for the monks of his day if their faces had not been tattooed with bright greens and reds.

Other men, always in pairs, followed them. Ishmael counted ten couples, and then there were none. But he was sure that the room in which they had chanted had held many more than that. The others must have gone off to other places or else were still in the chantry. But, if they were, they were silent.

He waited. The silence became a singing. The dark-ness settled as if it had substance and weight and a mindless, malign purpose. Once there was a clank from behind him and he jumped, along with the others. But it was the beast grating its stone claws against the steps in an effort to get onto its feet.

Namalee sniffed suddenly and put her nose to the end of a shaft and breathed deeply again. Then she said, "I thought I smelled it. It's the odor of the gods. The sacred room of worship must be very close indeed. But it might as well be a thousand miles away."

Ishmael sniffed but could detect nothing. However, he had not been brought up in the odor of sanctity and so lacked a trained nose. And if he did not soon track down the secret of unlocking the doorway to the next room, he would lack more than just a nose.

Ishmael listened but could hear nothing from the other side. He ordered that one torch be relighted. When the flame sprang out, causing him to blink with the light, he took the torch and held it so that its light fell through the length of a shaft. One by one, starting from the upper right-hand corner, he examined the interior of each shaft, searching for some difference in color of the stone, some lines, however faint, which might indicate a plate set in the hollow, or anything that was even in the slightest suspicious. But he found nothing.

He turned away from the wall to start an intense examination of the walls, the floor, and the ceiling adjacent to the wall.

As he did so, he heard a slight squeaking sound, and he whirled. Krashvanni, the man who held the bag of powder with which to put out the torch, reached out for his flame. But Namalee said, "The wall is moving!"

It was true. It was not turning upon a vertical pivot, as he would have expected. It was revolving on a horizontal rod, its lower part moving upward.

Ishmael prayed to all the gods that be, not forgetting Yojo, Queequeg's godlet, that no Booragangahns would happen by at this time.

Before the bottom of the wall had lifted more than a foot and a half, he was sliding forward on his chest. The others followed him, and long before the slow-moving section had turned completely over the band was in the little room on the other side.

"What caused it to move?" Namalee said.

"I do not know," Ishmael said. "But I strongly suspect that the activating mechanism is triggered by a bright light applied in a certain sequence to each of the shafts.

Perhaps there is no necessary sequence, or it may be that just a certain number have to be exposed to a bright light. I do not know. But I am sure that the key is the application of torchlight to something within the shafts. Perhaps the light sets up a chemical reaction analogous to that . . ."

He stopped. The tongue of Zalarapamtra had no words for the scientific inventions of Monsieur Daguerre or Professor Draper. Besides, what mattered was that he had accidentally discovered the lock, however it worked.

"Zoomashmarta is with us!" Namalee said. "He knows that we have come for him through terrible dangers, and he has shown us the way as a reward for our devotion!"

"That is an explanation which cannot be disproved," Ishmael said.

He sent two men into the corridor to the left to scout, and he led the others down the opposite corridor. This was a very short incline which led into a vast room carved out of a greenish rock with red stippling. Torches were everywhere, and the sweet and intoxicating perfume of the gods was heavy.

Cautiously, Ishmael stuck his head around the corner.

There were hundreds of altars cut out of the rock; in fan-shaped bowers squatted the gods, the great and the little.

Far down at the other end of the room, perhaps a hundred and fifty yards away, was the largest altar of all. On it sat the largest idol he had ever seen, though, admittedly, until then his experience with gods had been limited to the small ones of the whaling ships.

It was about two and a half feet high. It was ivory with red, black, and green streaks, and had many arms and two heads. It was Kashmangai, the great god of the Booragangahns.

A dozen robed priests were in the room. Three were genuflecting over and over before Kashmangai. The others were dusting the gods with feathery dusters or sweeping up the floor with feathery brooms.

Ishmael withdrew his head and became slightly dizzy with the movement. Even at this distance the perfume was strong enough to make him somewhat drunk.

"You'll have to identify Zoomashmarta and the lesser gods," he said to Namalee.

She looked around the corner for perhaps a minute and then said, "He and the small ones are on altars near the great one of Kashmangai."

The two scouts returned. They had traveled down the corridor to a point where it crossed another. They did not dare go further because of the sounds of many men nearby.

"This corridor could be a well-traveled one," Ishmael said. "So we'll have to act quickly."

He gave orders to each. The bowmen fitted arrows to the string and stepped out of the entrance. The others came behind them, and the entire band walked swiftly forward. They meant to get as close as possible before the priests would be aware of them. The bowmen had orders to shoot at the priests who were most distant.

The three before the great altar were still genuflecting. The cleaners had their backs to the band. Ishmael got within twenty feet of the nearest before the man turned around and saw them.

His eyes widened, his mouth fell open, his skin turned gray.

Ishmael was already in the act of throwing a spear he had borrowed from an archer. The point took the man in the open mouth and drove into the back of his throat. Gurgling, the man fell with a crash against an altar, knocking over a small idol.

The bow strings thrummed; the arrows leaped ahead and plunged into the backs of the three before Zoomashmarta.

Other arrows and spears struck the remaining priests. None were able to give loud cries.

Most of the priests had died; those who still breathed were unconscious and would probably remain so until they died. Their throats were cut, and the bodies were dragged out of sight behind various altars.

Ishmael went with Namalee to the altar where the Booragangahns kept Zoomashmarta and the lesser gods prisoner. The great one was a foot and a half high and had a fat Janus head with two faces. He was sitting cross-legged with one hand on his lap and the other raised with a jagged stick which represented lightning. The lesser gods were about a foot high. All exuded the overpoweringly sweet and overwhelmingly intoxicating perfume.

Ishmael felt by then as if he had had four cups of rum unmixed with water.

"We have to get out of here quickly," he said to Namalee. "Or I'll have to be carried out of here. Aren't you affected?"

"Yes, I feel very happy and a little dizzy," she said. "But I am used to the divine perspiration and so I can stay soberer for a long time."

Ishmael wondered how the priests endured the perfume and then thought that they would be like the drunkards of the ports, the men who could drink enough to put others under the table and still stagger along the street and beg, in a clear enough voice, for money with which to buy more drink.

The little gods and Zoomashmarta were put into the bags of skin which would contain much of their perfume. Ishmael, seeing that their primary goal was accomplished, gave the order to return.

But Namalee said, "No, we must steal Kashmangai and take him back with us."

"So that the Booragangahns will then retaliate?" Ishmael said. "Do you want to establish a seesaw of slaughter?"

"Gods are always stolen," Namalee said, astonished.

"Why not just drop Kashmangai into a dead sea and forget about him?"

"He would not like that," Namalee said. "He would not rest until he had seen to our complete destruction. But while we hold him prisoner, part of his power is ours, and ..."

Ishmael was about to throw up his hands in surrender and in disgust, when the scouts, who had stayed in the corridor as sentinels, came running.

"We had to shoot two priests," one said. "We tried to take them unaware and failed. One shouted out an alarm before he died, and now there is much commotion down the hall."

Kashmangai was stuffed into a bag, and the band started back toward the corridor. But, on reaching it, they saw a mob of priests and some armed men coming down the hall corridor toward them. Several had bows.

Ishmael snatched a torch from a man and ran down the short flight of steps to the wall with the shafts set in it. He passed the torch back and forth before each shaft in the same linear sequence he had used on the first occasion. The stone squeaked and the lower part of the wall started to swing out.

The approaching Booragangahns gave a great shout on seeing this, and two of the bowmen pushed to the front. They fitted arrows to their strings, but both fell before the shafts could be properly sent. Ishmael's archers had shot first.

At this, the entire enemy group ran forward, screaming war cries. Another volley of arrows downed those in front and then those immediately behind, and the others tripped on the bodies. Ishmael scooted under the wall with Namalee, carrying Zoomashmarta in a bag, behind him. A man carrying lesser gods followed her and close on his heels was a man carrying Kashmangai. Others followed them, rolling under the rising wall swiftly.

The wall revolved completely over, and the last man coming through, Ashagrimja, was caught by the edge of the descending part. He screamed out and two men grabbed his arms and pulled. But they were too late. The inexorable wall crushed his spine and continued to press through his body. Then the wall stopped, still open by several inches.

The enemy began to hack at the body to cut it apart and so let the wall continue to complete its revolution. Then they would unlock it again with their torches.

Two of Ishmael's archers shot through shafts, and though the arrows went at an upward angle, they struck two men. But an enemy archer got down on his side and sent an arrow underneath the wall. A man fell with an arrow in his ankle, and the god he was carrying crashed on the stone floor.

Before the wounded man could get up again, a spear shoved under the wall drove into his neck, and he died.

Ishmael shouted at his men to retreat. There was nothing to be gained by staying by the wall and much to lose. The hubbub outside was increasing. It was obvious that the whole temple and, for all he knew, the whole city, was alarmed by now. Even if his band wasn't followed through this wall, it might find itself cut off when it reached the boats. The Booragangahns would not take long to realize that the invaders had to have entered from the underside of the ledge. They would send boats and ships around under to cut them off. And they would also send ships out to look for the mother ship and her supporting war vessels.

Ishmael's only hope was to get away in the boats before the forces on the topside of the ledge were notified of what was going on.

He led the way down the steps with a torch in one hand. Namalee fell, slipped halfway down with the god and, screaming, slid down toward the stone beast.

The monster had somehow managed to turn over onto its feet. It was now climbing again with its lower hind feet braced on the fifth step up from the floor. On seeing Namalee fall, it shot its neck out and its jaws opened. The god in the bag, Zoomashmarta, bounced ahead of Namalee, rose into the air, and was snapped into the mouth of the stone beast.

Ishmael jumped down after Namalee, who had stopped sliding, and pulled her back up from a step just out of reach of the head. She was skinned bloodily on her knees and hands and her forehead, but otherwise she did not seem harmed.

The beast had closed its jaws on the idol of Zoomashmarta, but now it opened them again. The statue was jammed tight inside the neck where it opened into the mouth.

"We have to get the great god back!" Namalee wailed.

Ishmael did not curse. The situation was too perilous—and at the same time touched with absurdity—for him to express himself in mere cursing.

"I don't think that your god wants to leave," he said. "If he does, he is certainly acting peculiarly."

Up over the top of the steps, the priests were shouting and swearing. They were cutting away the body so the wall could descend and then be raised again.

Behind him were the silent survivors of his band.

Ahead was a stone beast that had swallowed divinity

134

but showed no sign of any transubstantiation or of any desire for communion other than with the flesh of the invaders.

And around him, permeating everything, was the sweet-stinking and drunk-making perfume.

If the influence increased, he would soon be seeing two stone beasts. And one was almost more than he could bear.

Karkri's body, he suddenly noticed, was gone. There was nothing left to show that he had existed except for streaks of drying blood on the steps. The beast had swallowed him without trouble.

Ishmael gave an order and staggered down the steps, stumbling once and almost falling. The great head with the unblinking dead eyes swung toward him, and the neck retracted as if getting ready to shoot out at him.

Nevertheless, it did not attack him, and he passed it safely.

Namalee followed him, but she was protesting that they could not leave Zoomashmarta behind.

"I am not another Tyr to put my hand into the monster's mouth and lose it!" Ishmael said. But the reference was, of course, lost on her.

"If we go ahead, we lose your god, that is true!" he shouted at her. "But if we stay and try to pry him loose, the Booragangahns will soon be with us! And then we die! So which is better? Die with your god or live without him?"

"Why couldn't it have been Kashmangai?" she wailed, weeping.

One of the men in the rear called, "The beast has swallowed Zoomashmarta! He is in the body of the beast now!"

Ishmael turned. All but three men had passed the monster. The last three were still on the steps, halted because the jaws were wide open and the extended neck was swinging back and forth.

There was little chance that all could get by the beast. The first to try it would be the sacrifice for the others.

Ishmael said, "Wait!" and he grabbed the bag containing Kashmangai from a man and threw it over the beast to the first man.

"Toss that into his mouth and then run by him!" he called.

"No!" Namalee cried. "We can't lose him, too!"

"Throw it!" Ishmael said. "We have no time to lose!"

The man, Poonkraji, swung the bag by its neck, and the bag and god were taken in by the great jaws. The three men scrambled by the beast. This time, as if catching a thought that had been traveling for a long time in the granite brain, the beast moved sidewise on its massive legs. Its shell caught the last man and crushed him against the wall.

"We can come back some other time and kill the beast and extract the two gods," Ishmael said. "The Booragangahns won't know that they are inside their guardian."

"But we have been defeated!" Namalee said. "This has all been for nothing!"

"Frustrated, not defeated," Ishmael replied. "But we will know something that the enemy does not, and we will return secretly and profit by it."

He did not believe that, since it was unlikely that the air shafts would be left open or unguarded from now on. But there was more than one way to enter a city.

They passed swiftly into the chamber of the things which hung from the ceiling by suction pads. They held their free hands by their necks as they dashed across the floor, the darkness burned away before them by the torches but reborn behind them. Pamkamshi and the two things had either been hauled up and eaten or else the path led them away from the bodies. They saw no sign of them during their flight.

Halfway across the room, they were attacked. Tentacles fell around them and others fell outside the group.

Ishmael rammed his torch against the one that looped around his neck and hand, and the tentacle withdrew.

Namalee cut at the tentacle encircling her with a knife. Four savage slashes half-severed the tough skin and muscles, and that tentacle coiled upward into the darkness.

There was the odor of burned flesh as other torches seared the tentacles.

The attack lasted less than a minute. Then they were free without losing a man.

Just as they started to run again, they heard a shout behind them. Ishmael whirled and saw torches flaring in the entrance far behind them. The Booragangahns had gotten through.

"Keep on running!" Ishmael shouted, and he turned and sped away.

When they reached the opposite door, over which a web was spun, they stopped. The torches of their enemies showed them struggling against the tentacles. Ishmael ordered the archers to shoot, and four of the pursuers, who were massed together while battling the tentacles, fell. Another volley downed four more, and the enemy broke and ran back to the entrance. But there they turned and fled yelling toward Ishmael's group again. A torch lit up the gray stone beast briefly as it rammed itself through the narrow opening with a scraping of stone against stone. Apparently it had swallowed the second god all the way and now was looking for mere humans as tidbits.

Ishmael, breaking through the web, wondered what mighty conflict between the tentacled, suction-padded creatures and the stone beast would ensue. He also wondered what had driven the beast to break through a doorway which evidently had always kept it in its narrow hall. Had the perfume of two mighty gods intoxicated it also, disturbing stone thoughts in a stone head, and perhaps making it drunk?

The band went at the same swift pace through the room housing the round creatures with the six legs. These swung down, one after the other, at thirty-second intervals, at the ends of their web-strands. But they did no injury to any except themselves. Torches struck them; knives slashed their legs or their strands from their backs. And soon the party was at the air shaft up which they had entered this unpleasant place.

While three archers stood guard—with only three arrows left apiece—the others went down the shaft. This took a long time because a boat had to be filled one by one and then pulled away with the crew lying on their backs. Then another boat had to be pushed under the shaft and this one filled. And the crew of this had to push another boat under.

Ishmael, as captain, waited until all were loaded aboard before he descended. He had expected the pursuers to show up long before the first boat was filled. Something had happened to stop them. He neither saw nor heard them, and he could only speculate that they had paused to fight the stone beast and so had given the tentacled things a chance to get at them.

As soon as his boat dropped away, the gas hissing as it discharged from the bladders, he dropped a signal overboard. Its fuse trailed a slight arc as it fell and then it blew up with a bright white glare that lasted for several seconds.

A minute later, something equally white burned in

138

the air several miles to the east. The first mate of the *Roolanga* had seen the flare go off under the ledge. He had attached one with a burning fuse to a small bladder. This soared up for a thousand feet before its compressed gas and explosive powder from a ground plant were set off.

Now the *Roolanga* should be rising to meet them, and the great ships above the city should be dropping swiftly.

The boats emerged from under the shadow of the ledge. Above them they saw lights dancing around the lip of the ledge. A row of lights slid out into their sight as a vessel moved out.

The alarm having been given, small boats would be setting out to curve around and under the projecting mass of rock.

A small wind suddenly pushed the boat. The loss of gas was stopped, and the masts were unfolded and set up. Then the arms were revolved and secured and the sails were unfurled. There was no moon, and the *Roolanga* was showing no lights. But the agreement was that the boats would meet them at a stated altitude and area after the first signal was released. The *Roolanga*, slowly rising, would also be moving northeast, close-hauled, for a while. Then it would turn and hope that this northwest course would bring it within visual distance of the boats. The big ship did not have much room for maneuvering after that. It would have to turn and sail close-hauled once more.

Ishmael watched the lights of the first vessel to leave the immense shadow that was the surface of the city of Booragangah. If it kept on its present course, it might run into the *Roolanga*. He looked upward but, of course, could not see the fleet of the Zalarapamtrans as yet. They would not be visible unless the moon appeared before they got close to the city. The moon was due to come over the horizon in about twenty minutes, if the sandglass clock could be trusted.

Ten minutes passed. Ishmael peered into the darkness and occasionally looked back and up. Three more lines of light had appeared. Four vessels were out cruising around, looking for the stealers of their gods. There would be others waiting in the docks, ready to shove out as soon as they saw the signal that they were needed.

Five more minutes went by.

"Where is she?" Ishmael muttered, and then he saw the vast dim shape. It was going northwest as they sailed southeast, and they were on a collision course.

Ishmael rattled out orders. A sailor opened a shutter in one side of a lantern-cage enclosing fireflies. The glow was not intense, but they were close enough. A minute later an eye of dull fire winked at them. Thereafter, signals were exchanged, and then the two began maneuvering so the boats could be taken overboard.

Before the first boat was taken in, the moon arose. A few minutes later a white light burned far up in the air, a signal from one of the Booragangahn ships. The lines of light began to turn toward the *Roolanga*, and a little later the vessels were easily visible in the shine of the moon. The *Roolanga* continued on its present course, northwest, until all the boats were received. Then it swung around, beating to the wind, until it was headed for a collision course with the four air ships.

But when the point of collision was only half a mile away, the *Roolanga* changed course again, the sailors working desperately to furl and unfurl the sails, and then the *Roolanga* was running free, the wind directly eastern.

Ishmael, looking back, saw the lights of four other vessels putting out from the slots on the edge of the great shelf. And then he saw a dark object coming down swiftly above the city, a tiny object visible only because the moon was up. That should be the giant fire-ship, the *Woobarangu*. It should be deserted by all except a few on the bridge, who were steering the ship to a spot above the center of the city. A minute or more, and the men on the bridge would climb aboard a boat and drift away. Shortly thereafter, fuses at various places in the giant vessel would burn down to the stores of flammable oil and low-energy explosives derived from the earth plants.

And then . . .

There it was!

The flame spread out and out, burning so fiercely that even at this distance Ishmael could see the vessel quite clearly. It fell more swiftly as the skins of the bladders were burned away and the gases escaped. The flames illuminated the city below, which was to Ishmael a mass without detail. But he knew that it consisted of a broad area about three miles square of flimsy houses and walks and stores and two levels, all supported by thousands of gas bladders. Here the majority of the population lived and worked, their houses anchored to the earth but almost entirely free of the constant trembling of the earth. The immense cigar shape was falling onto the center of the city, and the light skin and wooden structures would catch fire, and the fire would spread quickly.

The vessel struck. Flaming fragments flew far out as the mass tore through the houses and walks of the two levels and smashed into the rock of the ledge. The fire spread out even faster than he had envisioned. Within a few minutes, a large part of the center was burning.

From where he was, the fire was beautiful. But he could imagine the screaming and the running of the women and children and men caught in the flames and of those not yet caught. The images made him sick. But he reminded himself that these were the people who had lured the *kahamwoodoo* to destroy their enemies. And these were the people who would return to hunt down the last Zalarapamtran if they learned that they had failed the first time to kill every one. Nevertheless, it was impossible for him to be indifferent to what was happening in that distant and beautiful flame or to be happy, as the Zalarapamtrans were.

By the light he could see five more ships sliding out of the slots in the lip of the shelf. The enemy was attempting to get every vessel out before they all burned. Doubtless the air was swarming with small boats also trying to escape.

At that moment the other Zalarapamtran ships were illumined by the increasing flames. They were coming down swiftly, and they were being steered toward the outer parts of the city. A few minutes passed and then new fires broke out on their trail. They had dropped firebombs on the periphery.

Suddenly one of the Booragangahn ships leaving the dock began to burn. A Zalarapamtran had sailed above it and dropped a firebomb on it. The ship continued on out from the city, as the flaming vessel dropped and then broke in two and the two parts fell together down the face of the mountain.

Namalee suddenly gripped Ishmael's arm and pointed to starboard. Ishmael looked and saw ten tiny objects in the moonlight.

"They must be Booragangahn whaling ships or warships returning," she said.

"Time to cut and run," he said. "We've done what damage we can to the city."

He spoke to the first mate, who transmitted his order. In a short time, a small bladder to which was attached a signal-bomb was released from the *Roolanga*. Presently the white glow spread out a thousand feet above them. And the vessels above the city turned toward the *Roolanga*. The *Roolanga* continued on its course toward the approaching enemy ships. The moonlight was strong enough for Ishmael to see the two dozen warboats released from the ships. These were swift, streamlined vessels, each holding about eight men. They would attempt to intercept and board the *Roolanga* while the mother ships would attempt to lightly ram her. The business of ramming was a delicate and precarious one, because too heavy an impact would break up both vessels and too light an impact would result in some damage to both but also in the escape of the intended victim. And if the enemy did not succeed in its ramming, the boarders would be at the mercy of the boarded.

Ishmael did not care for this type of near-suicidal warfare. But there was nothing he could do to change it. He waited while the boarding boats, swifter than the great ship, came alongside and the harpoons were cast. These penetrated the thin skins and some came loose and others caught their barbed heads in catwalks or in the gas bladders. These immediately began to discharge, and the ships dropped. But the crew hastened to cut the lines loose and to slap a gluey compound over the rents and then a patch over the glue.

Meanwhile, the boats had launched the other harpoons, and these boats were swung inward against the sides of the ship, and the crew cut holes in the skins and climbed through.

The mother ship had dropped also as its antagonist dropped, but it did not fall swiftly enough, and it sailed just above the *Roolanga*, the bottom of its hull missing the top of the *Roolanga*'s. Its huge rudder did strike against the *Roolanga* near the bridge and tear out a huge hole in the hull. But at the same time its own rudder was severely damaged.

The *Roolanga* continued on her course and sailed between two enemy ships which almost collided after missing her. More boats attached themselves to the *Roolanga*, but the archers aboard shot the boarders, and the survivors scrambled back to their boats. There was no sense in their continuing to fight if the mother ships could not ram the *Roolanga*.

The enemy vessels turned to sail close-hauled while the *Roolanga* continued to beat to the wind. Presently, as time and the moon smiled down upon the Zalarapamtrans, the *Roolanga* turned and ran free. The others of the fleet were strung out behind the flagship for a mile. The enemy ships that had left the city turned again and quartered, but they had little chance of catching the Zalarapamtrans for a long time. The approaching fleet, having signaled the others with their firefly lanterns, changed course to intercept the enemy.

Even though the invaders were more heavily laden, bearing a cargo of firebombs which they had not had a chance to drop, they had a head start. Whether or not they could keep it was up to the fortunes of war and the wind. Ishmael did not give the order to unload the bombs and so enable them to run faster. He thought that the bombs might be used, and he was studying their possibilities.

The night wore on. The moon sank over the western horizon and blackness returned, relieved only by the running lights on the two fleets. Ishmael slept three times. The moon shone on the pursued and the pursuers six times. The sullenly red sun rose, and still the distance between the two, though narrowed, was wide enough so that Ishmael did not worry.

By then the damages to the hull had been repaired. And the ships had sailed three times through red-brit clouds and scooped up great quantities to increase the galley's stores and to feed the bladder-animals. The additional gas enabled the Zalarapamtran fleet to rise to a height of about twelve miles. The Booragangahns followed suit and then, as they slowly decreased the distance between them and the invaders with agonizing slowness, they also increased their altitude. At the end of the second day, they were about six thousand feet higher than the pursued.

However, since the air was thinner there, they began to lose speed. They had counted on encountering a stream of air with more velocity than that on a lower altitude, but this time the stream failed to appear. So the Booragangahns dropped back to an altitude about two hundred feet above the Zalarapamtrans.

The first mate commented that they would be overtaken before the next sun arose.

"I am planning on that," Ishmael said. "In fact, I have been thinking about deliberately allowing them to catch up with us. But if we were to reduce sail, we would make them suspicious and so cautious. My plans call for them to approach boldly and confidently. They outnumber us so much they must think that we stand little chance against them."

Poonjakee knew Ishmael's plan though, judging by his fleeting expression, he did not have much faith in it. That was not the way his fathers had fought in the air. But he said nothing. Anyone who could invade the enemy stronghold and steal back their god—though losing it later—and could then destroy the city with a weapon he had invented, was not a man to argue with.

Poonjakee's prediction was not quite accurate, but it was close enough. The Booragangahns did not catch up with them before the night was ended. An hour after the red sun came up, their lead ship was over the rear ship of the Zalarapamtrans. By then Ishmael had transmitted orders that all his ships should reduce sail so they could sail in side by side. The maneuver was executed swiftly enough, but the line was more ragged than he wished.

A moment after the ships had gotten into the formation ordered, and just after the enemy flagship was above its chosen antagonist, Ishmael got word of a new development.

The sailor who reported was scared. Not because of the impending battle, however, but because of what he saw dead ahead.

Ishmael turned and saw the vast purplish mass floating many miles ahead.

"That is the Purple Beast of the Stinging Death?" he said. "You are sure?"

"That is it," Namalee said, speaking for the sailor. She too was wide-eyed and pale-skinned.

That the enemy had also seen it was evident. The flagship abandoned its position above the other ship and retreated, reducing sail to do so.

"It is probably the Beast that killed my people," Namalee said.

She was guessing, but the creature could well be the same one. They were extremely rare, fortunately for humankind, and they did not move swiftly, if the lore of the Zalarapamtrans could be trusted. They often descended to the ground and fed on the creatures there. This one may have been doing so recently, because it was only about six thousand feet high, though rising.

Ishmael stood for a long time in thought. Poonjakee paced back and forth, looking sidewise at Ishmael and undoubtedly wondering why he did not order a change of course.

"The Booragangahns lured the Beast to Zalarapamtra," Ishmael said. "They were playing a very dangerous game, since the Beast, despite its immense size and weight, can be swift. It can propel itself by means of explosions, you say?"

"Yes, *Joognaja*," Poonjakee said. "Moreover, the *kahamwoodoo* can modify parts of its body to act as sails. It is as if it had a thousand and a thousand sails. And if it gets close enough to a ship, its tendrils shoot out and catch onto the ship, and it pulls the ship to it and then the tendrils seize the crew, and . . ."

"You must not continue to think about what it can do to us," Ishmael said. "You must concentrate on what we can do to it."

Ishmael gave no order to change course. Neither Poonjakee nor Namalee dared question him on this, though they were eager to hear what he had in mind. Ishmael watched the enemy fleet, which had dropped behind and veered away. Now all sails were being let out, and the ships were once more running free. Evidently their admiral had decided that the Zalarapamtrans were going to skirt as closely as possible to the Beast. In that manner, the Zalarapamtrans hoped to scare off their pursuers. But the Booraganganhs were not going to be scared off, though they were, doubtless, scared. Their grandmothers had frightened them with stories of the Beast when they were little children, and they had seen what the Beast could do when it settled over Zalarapamtra. Moreover, whaling ships had run across the Beast, and the few survivors had vividly described the results.

An hour passed. By then the creature looked like a floating island. It was a rough disk with a diameter of at least a mile and a half and a thickness of three hundred feet. It had no eyes or ears or mouths that Ishmael could see, but Namalee assured him that he would see the mouths soon enough. The body was purplish and the tentacles—most of them coiled now— were blood-red. The tentacles were on top and bottom of the thing. Its shape kept changing with depressions forming here and there and billowing at other places.

"It's rising but not very swiftly," Ishmael muttered. "It apparently does not care whether we are above or below it."

He looked back. By then the Zalarapamtrans must have been close to panic, wondering how closely he planned to sail before turning. They must also have been speculating that he hoped to turn in time to escape the Beast but to bring the pursuers into grave danger.

Ishmael gave no orders, not even to hold the ships steady. Their original order would stand until he countermanded it.

It was evident by then that if the ships did not shift course, they would sail above the Beast at a height of two hundred feet. And at the rate at which the Beast was climbing, it would be able to seize their ships long before the ships got to the other end. Even if the vessels increased their gas, they could not gain altitude as swiftly as the Beast. Nor was their admiral giving orders to feed the bladder-animals.

Namalee and Poonjakee were sweating, though the air was cold. The steersmen, also pale and wet, were biting their lips. None of them, as Ishmael knew, lacked courage. But this situation was something they had never experienced, and all their infant-born terrors were crawling out on the surface of their nerves, scratching and rasping.

Ishmael himself was far from being easy. This creature was indeed a kraken of the atmosphere but far more fearsome and deadly. It generated in him a feeling that something dark and unnatural had come from the evil areas of his own mind. It was a nightmare that had no right to exist in the flesh. Awakening should dissolve it, just as an evil dream evaporates when its generator awakens.

But this, despite its unnaturalness to Ishmael, was a natural being in a nightmare world. It was what the End of Time should spawn.

Ishmael remembered Ahab's words about a "six-inch blade to reach the fathom-deep life of the whale." Was he not trusting too much to the weapons he carried in these ships, weapons which might not have the devastating effect he had hoped for on this strange and largely unknown creature? If he, Ishmael, was wrong, then he had led all those who trusted him into death.

He looked back. The Booragangahns had quartered, probably with the intention of eventually beating to the wind.

Then Ishmael jumped, as did everybody on the bridge and, undoubtedly, every soul in the fleet.

A series of loud explosions broke loose from the monster. Flesh peeled back to reveal large round holes and the edges of some hard black substance, all looking very much like cannons. They spouted smoke and flame and noise, and the Beast moved swiftly to starboard. Then more smoke and noise, this time from the rear of the Beast, and it moved swiftly ahead into the wind.

Both fleets were above the center of the monster.

The purplish mass rose with sickening velocity as more explosions came. Ishmael could not see the smoke or flame from these because they came from the underside of the Beast. They were being used, like rockets, to propel the Beast upward.

Ishmael had not expected such demonic speed. The Beast was so huge and billowing that it had looked murderous but unwieldy. Now he saw why ships that ventured too closely, accidentally or otherwise, were so often lost. And he knew then that the Booragangahns, when luring the Beast to their enemies, must have paid a heavy price.

He rapped out his order and Poonjakee relayed it. Signals flashed; the sailors recovered their startled nerves and obeyed. The hatches in the bottom of the hull were opened, and the business of lighting the fuses and dropping the bombs through the hatches was begun.

The blood-red tentacles, however, were uncoiling. Their lower parts were lumpy, which meant, Ishmael supposed, that they were encased here and there with small gas bladders. This enabled the lower parts to unreel to at least fifty feet. The remaining portions were still coiled, waiting for the moment when they could snap out like whips.

Ishmael saw the black bombs with their red fuse-tips and pale gray smoke fall toward the billowing mass. The first landed on a patch of purplish skin near the base of a tentacle. It burned and then went off with a small bang. When the smoke had cleared, a large hole was revealed. There were great empty spaces inside the Beast crisscrossed by fragile lines of flesh or tissue. One egg-shaped end of a bladder protruded beyond a flap of skin.

Ishmael gave orders that the ship should discharge more gas and so bring it even more swiftly into direct contact with the monster. Poonjakee, looking as if he believed that Ishmael had lost his mind, transmitted the order.

The second bomb to burst was a firebomb. Its flaming oil spread out over the skin, burned it away and dropped into the interior. The interconnecting tissues and dark veins and arteries—or so Ishmael classified them—burned away. A bladder abruptly caught fire. And then the bladder exploded, and smoke and flames enveloped that part of the Beast directly below them.

Ishmael had not known what type of gas the Beast generated in its bladder until that moment. No one knew;

everybody had taken it for granted that the gas was nonflammable, as it was in the bladders of the ships.

Ishmael was not as happy at the discovery as he should have been, because the first of the tentacles had reached the ship. They gripped the masts and arms of the lower mast and went in through the open port where several boats were kept, and shortly thereafter other tentacles followed. These writhed around the area, found no sailors—they had all retreated before the tentacles got near the ship—and wrapped themselves around beams, girders, catwalks and masts.

The vessel was pulled downward as more tentacles gripped it. Smoke from the burning Beast poured into the open parts of the *Roolanga* and quickly filled it. The sailors, coughing, eyes streaming, fell at their posts, though some stumbled up ladders to the higher levels.

The bombardiers continued to light fuses and throw out the bombs. These exploded and sent oil spraying everywhere, some of it actually touching the ship. But the fire burned away only the skin it touched and then was extinguished.

Suddenly the ship rose. Its breakaway was so violent that many were thrown to the deck, and some with precarious holds on ladders or catwalks were thrown through the air and out through the thin skin of the hull or through the open spaces.

The fires had burned away the bases of the tentacles gripping the *Roolanga*.

The unloading of half of its bombs had lightened the ship considerably. It kept on rising until it had cleared the smoke. Ishmael saw that his other vessels had dropped many of their bombs, too. The Beast was burning in a hundred places; even as he watched, he saw another gas bladder explode with a violence that lifted the ship above it. The explosion also tore loose the tentacles that had gripped the lower mast, and that ship rose.

The Booragangahn fleet was enwrapped in tentacles. Each ship had been pulled downward until it was half-enfolded in billowing flesh. The lower masts had pierced the body of the Beast, but evidently this did not perturb it. Its tentacles were in every opening of every vessel, and several vessels were broken open when the Beast discharged some of its "cannons." Other tentacles poured into the shattered hulls.

Ishmael transmitted more orders to his fleet. Those that had gotten away were to descend and help their trapped fellows. His own ship tacked and discharged gas at the same time, sliding about fifty feet above one of their vessels, the *Mowkurree*, which had not been able to pull loose. More bombs were dropped, some of which exploded so close to the ship they tore apart beams and walkways or started fires on the skin. But the *Mowkurree* was released. Its fore lifted up first, the tentacles sliding off and then collapsing from it, and then the aft lifted, and the ship was free.

More great bladders exploded. A Booragangahn ship was released when an explosion blew up a part of the Beast immediately by the ship. It rose at an angle and then rolled over on its side. Its starboard masts had been broken off by the blast, and the weight of the port masts was tilting it. Little figures fell onto the Beast fifty feet below. Some sailors had lost their holds when the vessel rolled.

Ishmael did not waste any bombs on the crippled ship. It was out of the action. Though it could still probably put out boats, these would be filled with men eager to get away from this area, not to board enemy craft.

Namalee cried out, and Ishmael turned. She was staring at one of their ships, which had passed too low over a series of exploding bladders. One of the flaming cells had been cast upward and had struck the lower part of the ship. Fire spread quickly, since the bladder seemed to cling to the hull. One of the ship's bladders was burned away, and the ship fell aft end first into the inferno below. One boat escaped, only to be caught by two tentacles. These pulled downward; the boat tilted, turned upside down, and several men who had not had time to strap themselves in fell out. But they died only a minute ahead of their fellows. The boat was pulled down into the smoke and not seen thereafter.

Though the wind was twenty knots strong at this altitude, it could not carry the smoke away quickly enough. The Beast was lost to the *Roolanga* in the heavy black cloud. Ishmael brought the ship about and dropped it a hundred feet so that the smoke filled the ship and flames licked at it through the smoke. He could see nothing except destruction and so took the *Roolanga* northwest, close-hauled. Suddenly he was on the windward edge of the Beast and he could see what was happening. Two other Zalarapamtran vessels were above the smoke. The others, he presumed, were lost. So were all the Booragangahn ships, because none were in sight. There were about twelve boats with green skins, containing all that was left of the enemy.

"The Beast is dying!" Namalee said. She looked at Ishmael. "You did it! You did what none except Zalarapamtra has ever been able to do! You are a god!"

"I am a man," he said. "Others will be slaying their Beasts, once they know how to make firebombs."

"The Beast is not dead yet!" Poonjakee said hoarsely.

He pointed downward and they saw scores of pieces of the Beast flying up through the smoke. They were borne by small bladders and carried a dozen tentacles each.

The Beast, dying, had broken itself up into many parts, capable of independent action. They extended parts of their skin to form sails and crude rudders, and they came as one toward the *Roolanga*. These, perhaps, were the smaller animals supposed to accompany the Beast.

Ishmael gave orders that the archers should shoot at the bladders of the creatures. The spearmen should cast their spears. And then he waited with his spear.

Three of the creatures grabbed the end of the starboard yardarms and hauled themselves along them until they reached the hull. There, finding no entrances unguarded, they made their own. Flaps of skin opened on the sides to reveal lipless mouths with thousands of sharp triangular teeth. These bit at the skin of the hull until they tore open the tough but thin material. Then the purplish, pulsing, billowing bodies elongated, and their tentacles reached through the openings, gripping beams and catwalks, and they pulled themselves through.

Sailors met them, were seized by the tentacles, cut the tentacles, were gripped again, hauled yelling to the mouths, and their heads or arms were bitten off.

But others rammed their weapons into the mouths or punctured the bladders, which expelled the gas swiftly. Other sailors ran up with torches, which Ishmael had ordered lit, and thrust into the tentacles. These were burned away or writhed away, and the torches were stuck into the mouths of the creatures.

Abruptly the three were gone. They had pulled themselves back out and dropped off, acting as if they still had full gas bladders. Their tentacles writhing, they fell down into the smoke still pouring out from the huge dead mass of the Beast.

Other independent pieces of the Beast had attacked the *Roolanga* at other points. But these, though they had taken their toll, had been killed or repulsed. And the other Zalarapamtran ships had also gotten rid of their boarders.

Ishmael said to Poonjakee, "We will pick up the Booragangahns in the boats, if they will surrender. We will spare their lives and take them back to Booragangah."

"Are you sick?" Namalee cried. "Has the hideousness of the Beast overcome your senses? You would have us give mercy to those killers and return them unharmed to their people? So they can thrive and grow strong again and then come to Zalarapamtra one day and murder us all again?"

"I have been thinking for a long time, since the chase was long, and there was much time to think," Ishmael said. "The people of Zalarapamtra are very few. And though the people of Booragangah outnumber them, they are very few too. It will take generations to build their population back to where it was. Both people will be subject to raids, perhaps to extermination, by other peoples. Both will be unprotected when the whaling vessels put out to the air, since most of the male population will have to go out.

"But what if the two peoples combined their populations? What if they decide to live together, as one people, a new people, in one place? Won't that double their chances of survival? Won't—"

"It is unheard of!" Namalee and Poonjakee cried with one voice.

"Ah, but I am a new voice!" Ishmael said. "And I have said several things you have never heard of! And I will be saying more unheard-of things!"

"But the gods!" Namalee said. "What will Zoomashmarta say? How could he endure to share equally with Kashmangai?"

Ishmael smiled and said, "They are sharing equal quarters and the same fate now in the belly of the stone beast. Indeed, the stone beast may be the greatest of the gods, since he carries two great ones in his body.

"It was this swallowing of the two that gave me the idea of combining the two peoples. Let Zalarapamtran and Booragangahn live together, in peace, with a united front against enemies. Let them worship Zoomashmarta and Kashmangai together. Perhaps the stone beast will be a god higher than they. I do not know what its name is, but the Booragangahns must have one for it. Or, if not, let us give it a name. The gods have always had names which men have given them."

All except Time, Ishmael thought. There have been gods of time, but no name for Time itself. And he thought of that fierce and old man with the ivory leg and the lightning streak down his face and body. Old Ahab, whose doomed pursuit of the white beast with the wrinkled forehead and the crooked jaw had been more than just a desire for vengeance against a dumb animal.

"All visible objects, man, are but as pasteboard masks. But in each event—in the living act, the undoubted deed—there, some unknown but still unreasoning thing puts forth the moldings of its features from behind the unreasoning mask. If man will strike, strike through the mask!"

What the white whale had been to Ahab, he told himself again, time was to Ishmael.

And the six-inch blade striking to reach the fathom-deep life of the whale was man's mind striving to comprehend the nature of time and timelessness. It could not be done. It ended with the defeat of the quester, as Ahab's quest had ended. Man could only live as well as he could with the greatest beast, Time, and then go into timelessness, still wondering, still uncomprehending.

He looked up at the agonizingly slow sun, dying as all things must die. He looked at the great moon hurtling across the dark blue sky. It was falling, and though it might take a million years yet, it would surely meet the earth some day.

What then? An end to mankind. An end to all of nature as man knew it. An end to time as man knew it. Why keep fighting when the end was known?

Namalee, her eyes wide with the shock of his proposal to unite with their enemies, had moved closer to him. He put out an arm and drew her to him, though such intimacy in public was repugnant to her people. Poonjakee, embarrassed, turned his face away. The steersman looked upward.

She was soft and warm and in her was love and the promise of children.

And that is what keeps mankind going, Ishmael told himself. *Though it seems incredible, our children may some day find a way to go to other suns, young stars. And then, someday, when the bright young star is an old red star, to still others. They haven't done so, apparently, in the millions of years that have gone by. But with a million years left, or even half a million, or a quarter of a million, mankind has time to beat Time.*

There are a lot more
where this one came from!

ORDER your FREE catalog of ACE paperbacks here. We have hundreds of inexpensive
books where this one came from priced from
75¢ to $2.50. Now you can read all the books
you have always wanted to at tremendous
savings. Order your *free* catalog of ACE
paperbacks now.

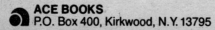 **ACE BOOKS**
P.O. Box 400, Kirkwood, N.Y. 13795

MORE TRADE SCIENCE FICTION

Ace Books is proud to publish these latest works by major SF authors in deluxe large format collectors' editions. Many are illustrated by top artists such as Alicia Austin, Esteban Maroto and Fernando.

Robert A. Heinlein	Expanded Universe	21883	$8.95
Frederik Pohl	Science Fiction: Studies in Film (illustrated)	75437	$6.95
Frank Herbert	Direct Descent (illustrated)	14897	$6.95
Harry G. Stine	The Space Enterprise (illustrated)	77742	$6.95
Ursula K. LeGuin and Virginia Kidd	Interfaces	37092	$5.95
Marion Zimmer Bradley	Survey Ship (illustrated)	79110	$6.95
Hal Clement	The Nitrogen Fix	58116	$6.95
Andre Norton	Voorloper	86609	$6.95
Orson Scott Card	Dragons of Light (illustrated)	16660	$7.95

FRED SABERHAGEN